THE WONDERLAND MURDERS

MILLIE RAVENSWORTH

1

The message on Penny's phone had read:

NANNA LEM'S BEEN TAKEN TO ST AGNES' HOSPITAL. SHE'S ASKED FOR YOU. IT'S CRITICAL. COME QUICKLY.

OF COURSE, Penny had to go. Firstly, there was that word 'critical'. Secondly, Nanna Lem, her last surviving and definitely favourite grandparent, had asked for her. Thirdly, the message had come from Penny's cousin, Izzy. This was Izzy, who rarely communicated with Penny beyond sending homemade birthday and Christmas cards and who surely wouldn't have broken that routine for anything other than an important reason. Fourthly, given that Penny's job at a

London hotel had recently come to a crashing end (for reasons she did not want to go into), she was very much at a loose end. All in all, it was a positive relief to be able to jump on a train at Liverpool Street Station and a little over an hour later to be on the streets of Ipswich in the rural East Anglian county of Suffolk.

St Agnes' was a small hospital on the edge of town, little more than a large house. It barely seemed like a hospital at all, and it struck Penny that it was an odd place to take someone in a critical condition.

The nurse took Penny through to a day room with huge supportive armchairs and a wide window that overlooked the shining River Orwell. Nanna Lem sat in an armchair inspecting a grape that she held between thumb and forefinger. Her left foot was in a support boot and raised on a cushion. She had a knitted blanket over her legs.

"What do you think of that, eh?" she asked, holding out the grape. "It's huge. No grape should be that big. They weren't that big in my day. It's not natural."

This did not appear to be a woman in a critical condition. A critical mood, perhaps, but nothing more.

"Morning, Nanna Lem," said Penny, and bent to kiss her. "I came as soon as I could."

"Oh, you shouldn't make a fuss over me," replied the old woman.

Nanna Lem was well into her eighties, and was of that breed of women that people tended to refer to as a 'tough old bird'. She'd lived her life on her feet: carrying bags of groceries up the hill to her house, peeling spuds at the kitchen sink, working behind the counter of the Cozy Crafts shop. Time might have weathered her leathery face and her hair might have turned to a cloud of wispy white, but Nanna Lem had always been a solid and dependable fixture in Penny's life, and hospitalisation didn't seem to have changed that.

As Penny sat, Nanna Lem offered her the bowl from her lap.

"Surprisingly large grape?"

"Er, no thank you. How are you?"

"Very well, thank you. Well, obviously not very but mostly. Well…"

And she eventually told Penny what had happened, which boiled down to the age-old truth that people above a certain age should not climb onto chairs to clean cobwebs from the ceiling. Or, indeed, for any other purpose.

"It's a sprain actually," she said, tilting her injured foot. "Or a bruised bone. Something like that. Not very serious."

"But you're in hospital," Penny pointed out.

"Ah, that's on account of me getting the white pills and the grey pills mixed up."

"Oh?"

"Should have been only taking one grey pill a day. Four of the white and one of the grey for the pain in my leg. Got all that the wrong way round and the grey ones made me feel very nice and one thing's led to another and the doctors tell me I've got opioid use disorder."

"Oh, my!" Penny exclaimed, which seemed to be the mildest possible response to the revelation that her Nanna was a drug addict.

"They've got me in here for at least a fortnight while I

come down or go cold turkey or something. And they've got me on some orange pills now which are just as nice."

They fell to chatting about everything and nothing. Uncle Harold's knee replacement. What Cousin Steven's youngest had been arrested for. How Cousin Debra had got herself a new place after the divorce and how she might or might not be living in sin with Gordon from the chippy.

"And how's London?" asked Nanna Lem.

"It's London," said Penny.

"I hear you're on a sabbatical."

Penny looked at her sharply, and then realised. "Did mum tell you that?" she asked. It was the lie Penny had told her own mother, who was half a country away in Nottingham.

"I assume that means you lost your job."

Penny chose neither to confirm nor to deny. She didn't need to.

"It's temporary," she said.

"Good."

"Good?"

Nanna Lem nodded emphatically. "You know I have the shop."

"Still?" asked Penny. Nanna's sewing shop, Cozy Crafts, was situated in the small market town of Framlingham, on the far side of Woodbridge and deep in rolling Suffolk farmland. "I thought Izzy had taken that over," she said.

Nanna Lem scoffed loudly. "I took her on to mind the counter and help me with some of the alterations work. You know our Izzy, not got the sense she was born with and can no more run a shop than a frog can drive a tractor."

"Oh. Oh," said Penny, for want of anything sensible to add. "I'm sorry to hear that."

She had to admit that this sounded exactly like the Izzy Penny remembered from her childhood. Izzy who had at various times in her youth set out to capture the mythical Black Dog of Bungay singlehandedly, navigate a pedalo to New Zealand, and prove that she could train a squirrel to perform circus tricks.

Nanna Lem reached forward with some difficulty and clasped Penny's hand.

"Which is why I want you to take over while I'm in here."

"Excuse me?"

"I would like you to take over Cozy Crafts."

Penny was stunned. This was not what she had envisaged for today. But what *had* she envisaged? Flying across the country to attend the bedside of a dying grandma? Tenderness and declarations of love? Muttered supportive comments for the other family members gathered round? This was... well, obviously, this situation was better. Nanna Lem wasn't dying, but... take over a shop?

"I know nothing about retail," said Penny.

"You worked in that hotel for best part of five years."

"That's hospitality."

"Do you know how to deal with customers?"

"Yes."

"Can you keep a place neat and tidy?"

"Of course."

"Can you handle money and invoices and know what to do with threatening letters that come in brown envelopes with little windows in them?"

"Yes."

"There you go then!" announced the old woman triumphantly.

"I can't actually sew," Penny pointed out.

"And that's what Izzy's for. She does the work. You run things. You can even use the flat above the shop since the rules won't allow you to stay in my place at Miller Fields. But it's only going to be for a short while. I did ask you to come and you came."

"I did," Penny admitted.

And that, it seemed, was that.

2

Three hours later, Penny stood in Framlingham marketplace and turned slowly around.

She was stiff from a lengthy bus journey. London to Ipswich had been a straight and speedy trip by train, fields and trees whizzing smoothly by, the only annoyance the man sharing her table and insisting on taking up most of it with his laptop. From Ipswich to Framlingham had been slow and winding, the bus stuck for fifteen minutes behind a pair of horses that had escaped from a field. Public transport in Suffolk required patience and a willingness to accept that rural bus services weren't quite the same as London ones.

It had been many years since she had last stood here. Her mum's side of the family had moved north years before, and it was only the occasional visit to see Nanna Lem or to attend the wedding of an old school friend that had brought her back.

She was surprised how much she had forgotten the appeal of this town. Shops and businesses occupied historic buildings all around the marketplace. If shops were people, the elegant Georgian townhouses would be cool middle-aged women, austere and immaculate. The black and white timber-framed buildings were jolly old women, a little wonky but comfortable in their own skin. The Victorian buildings, in contrast, plucked design features from many different places, like canny fashion students.

This seemingly sleepy Suffolk town was one of those places that appeared to have grown by accumulation rather than any form of planning. Ancient stonework supported masonry that was merely old. The overall effect was a space dotted with archways, back alleys and shadowy dead ends. A little way up one side street was the old church she vaguely remembered from childhood visits, and further along, the grand medieval castle that brought tourists to the town.

Memories of all of this came flooding back. What didn't come immediately flooding back was a memory of where Nanna Lem's shop actually was. Memories were annoyingly impressionistic like that; the maps of childhood and nostalgia didn't come with conveniently-labelled street names or door numbers.

Penny's wanderings led her up by the side of a shop until she found herself in a courtyard area that ended with the open doorway of Framlingham Town Library. Instantly equating libraries with knowledge and information, she went inside to ask if they could direct her to Nanna Lem's shop.

Set in a grand two storey building, Framlingham's library was one large open room with some other rooms off to the side. Penny barely remembered it from her childhood but supposed she must have been in here before. Non-fiction was tucked in one of the side rooms. Grey shelving screened off and subdivided the adult reading section. Lower tubs of books were scattered around the children's section. And, above the reading chairs and study tables, there were colourful displays about favoured books and upcoming events.

The older woman at the counter by the door had a slender figure and ash blonde hair.

"You look lost," she said.

"You're absolutely right," said Penny. "I'm looking for a shop in the town."

"This is a library," she pointed out, and smiled to indicate she knew that Penny knew what it was.

"A shop called *Cozy Crafts*," said Penny.

"Oh, you probably walked right past it to come here," replied the librarian.

"I feared as much."

"After a fancy dress outfit?"

"Er, no. I'm actually helping out. It's my Nanna's place."

"Lemmy?" The woman frowned. "I heard she was in the hospital."

"Hence me," said Penny.

"I do hope she's recovering well? Know a lot about fancy dress, do you?"

"I thought it was a sewing shop."

"A bit of this, a bit of that."

A man in a drab suit that made him appear older than his middling years approached, tapping away on a computer tablet. "Lorina, the book group selection in back should have been sent back to central last week," he announced.

"I'm talking to a visitor, Roy," the woman said.

Only then did the man seem to notice Penny. He blinked like a lizard emerging from under its stone.

"You can chit-chat to friends later," he said.

"A library visitor," replied Lorina the librarian.

"Service users is the preferred nomenclature," said Roy. "I apologise," he added, to Penny.

"Do you?" Penny said, coolly. She had no idea what the working relationship was between these two, but only one of them had interrupted a conversation and called her a 'service user'.

The librarian looked at him with equal coolness and said, "I will finish my conversation with..."

"Penny," said Penny.

"Penny," continued the librarian, Lorina, "and then I might possibly maybe take a look at the book group returns."

Roy seemed entirely unhappy with this decision, but sniffed, looked at his tablet and moved off.

"Ignore Roy," said the librarian once he was gone. "It's a built-in hazard of having the library service area manager living only two streets away from the library, but it's my final week on the job and there's nothing he can do."

"I see," said Penny. "Um, the shop."

"Cozy Crafts. Yes. You need to go back onto the market place, turn left and it's there on your left two, no three, doors along. If you reach Thumbskill's jigsaw shop, you've gone too far."

"I really hadn't noticed," said Penny.

"Well, yes. Unlike someone's house which is painted an illegally garish shade of pink" — she cricked her head in the direction of the departing Roy — "Lemmy's shop doesn't really make its presence felt. But it's there, I assure you."

"Thank you," said Penny. "Can you really have an illegal shade of pink?"

"You can if it's a listed building," replied Lorina, darkly.

Penny thanked her again and moved to leave.

"I might pop in later," Lorina called after her. "I need a costume for World Book Day."

"Oh," said Penny, not sure if she wanted fresh custom before she'd even seen the shop. "I'll... I'll look out for you."

She left the library, followed the directions she had been given, and as promised, there was the shop.

The words *Cozy Crafts* were painted above the large bay window, but they had faded and peeled until the lettering was merely one shade lighter than the white woodwork behind it.

She moved closer to the window and peered inside. It was a spacious shop, and she could see display shelving, but from here, she still couldn't tell what it sold. The Georgian windows were large. It would be beautifully light and airy inside.

She opened the door and a gentle chime jangled above her.

3

The floorboards of the shop, the shelves that lined the walls and the desk for the till were all made from the same dark wood. Penny ran her fingers along the ancient grain of a shelf and wondered whether this shop had an intriguing history. An antique sewing machine on a twirly iron stand was on display behind the window, and a large flat table stood in the centre of the room. Nobody stood at the till, in fact it looked as if the shop was empty.

A clattering noise announced the arrival of a woman descending the staircase opposite the till. She wore loose harem pants and a tie-dye t-shirt.

This was Cousin Izzy. There was no mistaking Cousin Izzy. She had a round face, a friendly face, made all the rounder by the shaggy bob haircut she wore. The friendliness was offset by the mild panic that hovered in her wide eyes. She always, Penny remembered, had a bit of the rabbit-in-headlights look about her or, indeed, as Nanna

Lem had perhaps more accurately said, the look of a frog at the wheel of a tractor.

"Hi, Izzy," said Penny. "It's me."

"So, it is," replied Izzy happily, giving no indication that she actually recognised Penny until she actually came forward and hugged her. "I knew you'd be coming."

"Nanna Lem tell you?"

"Read it in my horoscopes."

"Ah."

"Come to help out for a bit?" she suggested.

Penny nodded. "Yes. Apparently." She lifted her small suitcase. "Came as a bit of a surprise to me."

"Well, you're here now. Cup of tea?"

"Oh, that's a great idea. I've had a long journey."

"Life is a long and mysterious journey with many turns."

"Yes," said Penny slowly. "But I've also actually had an actually long journey to actually get here."

"A journey of a thousand miles starts with but a single step."

"Actually, the eight fifteen from Liverpool Street."

"And ends with a toddle up the stairs cos that's where the kettle is."

Following Izzy up the stairs, Penny paused for a moment and turned around to absorb what the shop looked like. The bones of the place were exquisite. Dark wood fittings, lots of natural light. From up here, though, she could see a good deal of dust, which wasn't a good look. There was something else that wasn't right, and it took Penny a moment to realise what it was.

"Hey, Izzy. I'm confused about something. If this is a sewing shop, where's all the fabric and stuff?"

Penny knew that there was a better word than 'stuff'. She had a lot to learn.

"Oh yeah, Lems and I had a chat about diversification. Do you know how much the mark-up is on some of the imported fancy dress stuff you can get?"

Penny realised that Izzy was talking about Nanna Lem. The nickname 'Lems' made her sound as though she should be fronting a heavy metal band.

"Yeah? I'll need to understand all that, I guess," said Penny. "Tell me if I'm wrong though, but it's not just about mark-up, is it? Some of it must be about how much you can sell. I can't help seeing a lot of dust in here. What are the takings like?"

"Takings, yeah. We can have a look," muttered Izzy.

Penny followed her into the upstairs room, where there was, indeed, a kettle. And a sink. It was next door to a room that had those amazing windows overlooking the square. Penny went over to look down. People hurried back and forth between most of the other shops, but very few spared a glance at the tired, faded facade of Cozy Crafts.

"What's this space used for?" asked Penny, looking around. It was a jumble of boxes and fabric rolls, but there were several tables and sewing machines visible between the mess.

"Lems used to run sewing groups in here, back in the day," said Izzy. "It's one of the places that needs a clear-out though."

"One of the places," echoed Penny. It sounded ominous.

Izzy handed her a mug of tea and grinned. "Yes. This place has three floors. Well, four if you count the cellar. The shop floor is the tidiest. The others need some work."

Izzy's words had Penny heading straight upstairs to the top floor. Nanna Lem had promised her the use of a flat. She urgently needed to understand how much work would be involved in creating a space where she could spend the night.

The elegant wooden staircase went all the way to the top floor, although the ceilings were not so high up here. Penny quickly discovered that there were three smaller rooms on the top floor. One was a replica of the workshop room below, piled up with similar amounts of mess. There was another room to the side with a sink and a small bathroom and then a closed door at the furthest point. Penny pushed it open and came face with – with *something*. She wasn't entirely certain what it was she was looking at. It looked like a curtain that she might brush aside, but it wasn't. It was an impenetrable wall of stacked fabric that was taller than a person.

"Hey, Izzy? This room up here, the one that looks like it's been filled with a bulldozer? Is this where my bed is?"

Izzy's head appeared at the top of the stairs. "Yes. You might need a bit of a tidy up."

Penny gazed at the scale of the job. Izzy's words really didn't begin to do it justice.

"It will be fun to have a bit of a sort through," continued Izzy. She pulled out a cardboard box that had been wedged in at the bottom and then lifted a bolt of fabric from the mass of materials. "See here? Each one should have a label on the end that tells you what sort of fabric it is. Your education can start right away. This one here is cotton lawn."

Penny shook her head. "Lawn?"

"It's really fine woven cotton. Feel it, it's gorgeous."

Izzy unravelled some fabric so that Penny could feel the drape and the weight on her hand. Right now, she didn't really care what was blocking access to her bed, as long as it wasn't there when she needed to sleep. She reached over with her other hand to stroke it. It was surprisingly pleasant.

"Ooh, it's lovely and light."

"Perfect for a summery blouse or dress," said Izzy, rolling it away again. "I'll teach you the types of fabric, but the best thing for now is to just get a feel for them. Wools, cottons, linens and silks are natural fibres, most of the things that sound like science experiments are man-made fibres."

Penny gently lifted a corner of fabric and held it against her cheek. "Oh, it feels wonderful."

"We'll make a fabric addict out of you soon enough."

Penny pulled out bolts of fabric and moved them to the workshop room on the top floor. As she uncovered random bits of useless clutter she dropped them into a box at the top of the stairs. There were mysterious broken tools, tiny bits of haberdashery trim and things that really belonged in the cupboard under the kitchen sink. The trouble with that was that she hadn't yet found a kitchen sink. Penny threw an ancient packet of rat poison into the box with a shake of her head. Mysterious foam objects called 'beauty forms' went in the box with it, so that Penny could ask Izzy what they might be.

Carrying rolls on the brief journey down the passageway gave her a chance to check out each fabric, opening out a few inches to examine the feel of it, and to see what the pattern and weave looked like. Some had no weave at all, like the stuff that Izzy informed her was tulle, pronounced 'tool'.

There was the jangle of the shop door opening downstairs.

"Maybe you can sort out these fabrics and I'll see to the customer," said Penny.

Izzy gave her a concerned look. "Do you know how to deal with customers?"

Penny grinned. "More than four years' experience in the hotel trade," she said confidently.

"Yes, but that was working with Londoners."

Penny picked up the box of dusty junk that was surely destined for the bin and hurried downstairs.

4

"Hello again!"

It was Lorina, the soon-to-be-retired librarian.

"Oh hi, nice to see you." Penny smiled, both because she already liked Lorina based on their earlier chat, but also because her first customer was a familiar face. It was a day of new experiences, and she was grateful for any crumb of comfort that she belonged in this place.

"I said I might pop in."

Penny put the box of junk down on the counter. "You did. Hadn't expected you so soon."

"Well, I am very interested in commissioning an outfit from you."

"For World Book Day, you said."

"Indeed." Lorina placed an old-fashioned handbag onto the counter, unclasped the top and pulled out several sheets of paper. "These should be helpful as a reference. I would like an Alice in Wonderland."

Before Penny took the papers from her, she thought for a moment. "Have you looked through the ready-made fancy dress outfits? I'm not sure if there might be an Alice in Wonderland one there? It could save you a lot of money."

Lorina held up a hand. "Let me underline the most important point of all with respect to this piece of work. I am constantly reminded that people have lost sight of the fact that World Book Day has the word 'book' in its title. I find it very trying when we are besieged with Spiderman and Elsa from Frozen costumes."

"I'm sure they appear in books of some sort," Penny hazarded.

"Literature originates in books. I'm not interested in novelisations, spin offs, tie-ins or any gross commercialisation of the written word. I must absolutely insist that we avoid any Disneyfication."

"Ah, I see."

"The Alice in Wonderland that I wish to emulate is the one from John Tenniel's original illustrations of Lewis Carroll's books. I have brought some prints for that very reason."

She laid out the pictures for Penny to see.

"Nice," said Penny, not certain what was expected of her.

"Full of period detail, as you can see," said Lorina.

Penny nodded wisely, peering at the illustrations which showed a much more thoughtful version of Alice than the Bambi-eyed Disney character. "These illustrations are all in black and white."

"They are."

"What do you want to do about colour?"

"Good question," said Lorina. "The usual interpretations of pale blue with white and perhaps yellow would be most appropriate, I feel. It must be blue. It's my favourite colour."

Penny went behind the counter to find something to write on. "Let me capture some details from you so that we can create a quote." She realised she had absolutely no idea how much they would be charging for the dress. "I'll need your contact details and of course the deadline you're looking at."

"Of course." Lorina jotted down her details.

"And I suppose, I should get some measurements from you now," said Penny. "I'll find a tape measure and we'll measure your chest, waist and back length."

"Bust," said Lorina.

"And your bust, yes."

"I mean we would call it bust rather than chest because I am a woman," explained Lorina.

Penny realised her mistake. "Oh gosh yes, of course. Although Alice herself was a girl, no?"

Penny saw that Lorina was not paying attention. She was instead staring at the junk box Penny had placed on the counter.

"Well, this is most intriguing!" she said as she walked over. "Might I take a closer look?"

"Er, sure."

Lorina lifted out a small but elegantly long-necked bottle. It was made out of blue glass with gold trim.

"I like this," she said.

"We're just have a clear-out upstairs."

"Are you? Well, this would be really good as a 'drink me' bottle."

"Pardon?"

"A 'drink me' bottle. For the Alice in Wonderland display we're making at the library."

"Oh. Oh, yes, I see that." She had only the sketchiest memories of the Alice in Wonderland story. There was, she knew, something about a girl shrinking and growing with everything she ate or drank. And a Mad Hatter. She wouldn't be telling Lorina that all those memories came from a certain Disney version of the tale. What she did say was, "You are welcome to take anything that interests you from that box, if you'd like to."

"Thank you, Penny." Lorina held the bottle up to the light. "Perfect."

"So, pale blue cotton for the dress, perhaps?" said Penny, checking that she had captured all of the order details. "I think we might have some. One moment and I'll take a look."

She went upstairs to check the fabric. Izzy had started stacking bolts of fabric along the landing wall.

"Have we got a sort of pale blue fabric for making an Alice in Wonderland dress?" Penny asked.

Without hesitation, Izzy reached in deep and pulled out a subtle fabric.

"A nice blue seersucker?" she suggested.

"Seersucker? Isn't that some sort of crepe fabric?" asked Penny.

"It's cotton, striped in slight crinkles. Looks smooth but feels cool on the skin."

Penny inspected it closer. It was a perfect pale blue.

"This will do just fine," she said.

"Great news," said Izzy. "If we use some fabric for this, we'll have the room cleared in no time."

Penny thought that there must be a word for the blindness that Izzy had to the scale of the problem. In the same way that most human brains couldn't easily picture the difference between a million and a billion, Izzy was incapable of seeing that the task of creating a liveable space from the chaos of the room as it currently stood, was way beyond the trifling amount of fabric that would be needed for an Alice dress.

Penny carried the fabric downstairs.

"What do you think?" She placed it carefully on the large flat table in the middle of the shop. She realised that this table was here to cut fabric, as she was able to lay the bolt down and unroll some of it for Lorina to inspect.

"You have a very good eye!"

"Um, thank you."

"This is truly delightful. Nice quality vintage as well, by the looks of the label."

Penny had to agree with Lorina. The label on the end did not look like anything that had been printed in the twenty-first century. She wondered how old the contents of Nana Lem's shop actually were.

"And the quote?" said Lorina as Penny hesitantly took her measurements.

"I will need to consult with, er, my colleague."

"Colleague?" said Lorina archly, and Penny guessed Lorina knew she meant Izzy. "I tell you what, if you're free, pop over to the library at five this evening. We're having some pre-retirement drinks, me and my fellow librarians. I'll introduce you to some people."

Penny thought that sounded perfectly pleasant. "Five o'clock. Drinks at the library. Quote." Penny nodded in agreement.

As the door tinkled to signal Lorina's exit, Penny let loose a sigh of relief. She had managed to put on a convincing display of competence, even though she realised she was clearly out of her depth in the world of dress-making.

5

Penny assisted Izzy with clearing out the room, explaining Lorina's commission as she did.

"You've got the measurements," said Izzy. "You'll probably need to create a toile."

"A what?"

"A toile."

"What's a toile?"

"Like a test piece, using something cheap to get the size right."

"Oh." That made sense. Izzy had said '*you'll*' need to make a toile. Penny was hoping her cousin realised that she would need to do all the actual dressmaking work.

The pair of them spent several hours removing things from the room. When they uncovered the corner of a bed, Penny felt spurred on to persevere. She still had no real idea what might lie beyond this point, but she had uncovered real signs of a bed and a small space next to it, and if it wasn't exactly comfort, it was at least a start. It would enable her to sleep tonight and for that she was grateful.

"Can I say something rude?" asked Izzy.

"Um," said Penny and then looked at her cousin. "Well, I suppose you'll have to now that you've asked."

Izzy composed her face. "I don't understand why Lems felt she needed to ask you to help out here. Things are ticking along just fine as they are, and I didn't think she was going to be in the hospital that long. No offence meant."

"None taken," replied Penny honestly. "I was as surprised as you. I thought I was rushing to the bedside of a dying woman."

"She's dying?"

"No. I thought that. She seems as strong as an ox, but your text said she was critical."

"She can be very critical," Izzy agreed.

Penny stared and then shook her head. "I think Nanna Lem just wanted me to help out. Take a look at this place with fresh eyes. It's like this crazy stockroom that should be a bedroom. I mean, when was the last time you saw this room empty?"

"Oh, I've never seen it empty. It's always had bits and pieces of old stock in it."

"Wow, that's crazy. Silly question, but can material go off?"

"Don't let Lems hear you calling it material, Penny. It's fabric. As for it going off, there are some things that can degrade. Elastic will perish, for example. Some sorts of silk become very fragile and brittle with age, but the rest should be fine if it's stored correctly."

"And by 'stored correctly' we obviously mean that it's made into a giant mound in what ought to be a living space."

Izzy gave Penny a sympathetic look. "You do need to carve out some personal space."

"And actually find some sheets to go on the bed, perhaps."

"I suppose so," said Izzy, as if this were an entirely secondary goal.

A few minutes later, Penny crowed with joy as she opened a trunk that contained sheets, blankets and pillowcases. "Bedlinen! It's possible that I'll get to sleep here tonight after all."

They pulled the items out, piling them on the bed so that Penny could choose the ones she wanted to use.

"These are made from linen," said Izzy. "It will be lovely to sleep in linen, very crisp and smooth against the skin."

"What's happened here, though?" Penny pulled out some pillowcases with delicate yellow flowers embroidered on the crispy white linen, but there were small spots of brown.

"Oh, rust spots, that's a shame," said Izzy. "It happens sometimes, not sure if tiny bits of iron get on them in the laundry or something. I tell you what, though...I have an idea for those."

"There are plenty of other pillowcases, what are you thinking?"

Izzy laid them out on the bed and tried some different arrangements. "The fabric and the embroidery are so nice, I bet we can use these to make Alice's lovely ruffled apron. These yellow flowers will look great on top of the blue dress, and we can cut away the stains in the bits we don't use."

How could Izzy see these possibilities in a handful of stained pillowcases? Penny tried to picture an apron hidden within the pillowcases. "I can't see it. Am I fabric blind or something?"

"No," Izzy laughed. "I'll show you later. I bet we can make it work. Let's make your bed up, so you can say that you've moved in. You'll probably want a quiet night after your first day."

"Actually, we've got an invite to Lorina's leaving drinks at five."

"Lorina the librarian?"

"Lovely Lorina the librarian."

"I didn't know you knew her."

"I don't," said Penny. "She did it on a whim. I get the impression that impending retirement is making her whimsical. This is an older woman who wants to dress up as Alice, after all. Coming?"

"Er, no," said Izzy. "I've got an editorial meeting at the Frambeat Gazette later this evening."

"The Fram what?"

"Frambeat Gazette," repeated Izzy. "It's a proper local paper. Not one of them things full of adverts that they slap your town name on but really it all comes from a nameless office in Ipswich or Colchester."

"Wow, many strings to your bow, huh?"

"Reckon they might want me to do a picture feature of Arabella Dinktrout. It's been on the cards for a while."

The name was familiar, and after a moment, Penny remembered why. Dinktrout Nurseries was one of the larger businesses in the area. Maybe this Arabella was heir to the Dinktrout fortune.

There was sudden concern on Izzy's face. "But you'll be okay?" she said.

"Okay?"

"At the party? Without me to hold your hand?"

Penny gave her a polite smile. "I'm a big girl now. I'll be fine. What could go wrong?"

_____

6

Penny entered the library.

"They're closed now," said a sixty-something woman with spikey hair who was standing beside the front counter. She was holding the hand of a young girl in a pretty dress.

"Lorina invited me," said Penny. "The drinks?"

"Ah." The woman smiled. "Then you are very welcome. I'm Pam Ockenden. My Annalise is the head librarian here."

Penny looked at the little girl afresh. Penny was not a great judge of the ages of children. She had none of her own, neither did any of her friends back in London, and she had not perhaps shown much interest in the lives of her many nephews and nieces. But even from a position of relative ignorance, she thought this child was surely too young to be a librarian of any sort, much less a head one. She frowned. Pam saw her confusion and laughed.

"No. This is Merida. Annalise's daughter. My granddaughter."

"Ah!" Penny bent down to address the girl, Merida. "And how old are you?"

"Ten," said Merida. "Are you short-sighted?"

Penny frowned again. Merida gestured to Penny's bent position.

"Ah, a little unnecessary," Penny agreed.

"And condescending," added Merida.

"It's apparently our word of the week," said Pam with an apologetic look. "Quite a vocabulary, our Merida has. I believe drinks are that way and up the stairs. We'll join you soon."

Penny wandered through the indicated room, where she found her way blocked by a tanned silver-haired man in a tartan flannel shirt who was browsing the shelves.

"I think they're closed now," said Penny to draw his attention.

He looked up. "Oh. I'm here for the after hours drinks."

"But perusing the shelves?" said Penny.

"Ah. I have a keen interest in local history." He stood up straight. "Stuart Dinktrout."

Penny nodded. "Of Dinktrout Nurseries?"

"Sole proprietor," he nodded back. "Home of the world famous Dinktrout Rose."

Penny remembered what Izzy had been talking about. "Ah, yes. Izzy mentioned something about your, er, Arabella, was it?"

"Love of my life," he said, and stretched to his full height, rolling his shoulders in that manner that supremely confident or indeed over-confident men tended to have. "Obviously, she's an absolute pig," he laughed. "She'll eat me out of house and home."

"Er, right," said Penny, not at all happy to hear a man talk about his wife, or maybe girlfriend, or possibly even daughter, in such terms. "I'm Penny. I'm looking after Cozy Crafts while my nanna is in hospital."

"Ah! Good!" he said, his eyes lighting up. "I must have a word with you, in my capacity as chair of the local chamber of commerce."

"Oh. That would be nice. I'm always keen to discuss business matters."

"And that dreadfully shabby façade on the front of your shop. Letting down the charming and rustic character of the town."

"Oh. Oh, I see."

"I've offered — your grandmother, did you say? — I've offered to have my man Aubrey come round and give it a lick of paint, but she always refused."

"I'm not sure what budget we've got for redecorating."

"I'll have him do it for free, gratis, on the house."

Penny hurriedly gave the offer some thought. A free paint job for the front of the shop? Perhaps to include the wooden window frames of the upper floors if she asked politely? To her mind, the only barrier was this Dinktrout man, with his somewhat overbearing manner and his despicable attitude to his lovely Arabella.

"That sounds lovely," she said, carefully.

"Good. Brilliant white, obviously. To maintain the local aesthetic."

"I don't have a problem with that."

"Superb!" He stood back to let her pass, as if she had finally passed a test and could now proceed to the party and the drinks. "Been here before?" he asked.

She looked at the turning corridor ahead. "Er, no. Not since I was knee high to a grasshopper, at least."

"This place used to be the old courthouse. That's the prison cell right in front of you. Used as an office by Citizens' Advice Bureau these days. You want to turn left, up the crooked stairs and into the old court at the top."

Penny did as told, and found herself in a brightly painted space filled with decorative book displays. Light entered through stained glass panels set into a raised ceiling above.

There was a little table set out with half a dozen glasses of fruit juice. Well, this was farewell drinks in a library, after all. Penny supposed she couldn't have expected champagne cocktails.

The only people present were two women. One was Lorina. Beside her was an attractive woman with chestnut hair and freckles. A second's look was enough to tell Penny this was undoubtedly Annalise, the daughter of Pam Ockenden and mother of the precociously pleasant Merida, the girl Penny had just met. The head librarian was clearly her mother's daughter and her daughter's mother, a genetic jigsaw piece that fit snugly between the other two.

Lorina saw Penny and beamed in delight. "Penny! So glad you could make it!"

"How could I turn down an invite from my currently favourite customer?"

The older woman swept round the table and took Penny

by the arm. "Let me show you the Alice in Wonderland display!"

Lorina steered her to a corner where carefully cut-out letters spelled out 'Alice in Wonderland' on the wall, so that nobody could be in any doubt as to the central theme. The display itself featured all sorts of themes from the book.

"Look here, we have a beautiful old copy of the book. It's from 1887."

Penny peered into a glass case where the book was open. It was a mellow, aged off-white colour, but the page was unmarked. The illustration showed Alice meeting the King and Queen of Hearts. Penny thought that Alice looked very much as if she was holding her own during the encounter. Her stance was assertive as the haughty, oversized queen pointed at her.

"It's lovely," said Penny. "I bet it's valuable, too?"

"I think it probably is. Ipswich hold it in their special collection, but we've borrowed it from them for this display."

Penny found herself examining Alice's dress in the picture. The blue dress flared charmingly at the hem. How would Izzy make that happen? She was putting all her faith in Izzy's ability to get this outfit right, but she really had no idea if her cousin could do it or not.

She turned her attention to the other items in the display. Lorina had added a charming 'drink me' label to the little blue bottle. There was a plate of porcelain cakes with an 'eat me' label, as well. There were motifs including a large teapot, a croquet set and a top hat all artfully arranged on an undulating piece of astroturf. As Penny moved on, there was an information board with all of the main characters and their roles explained.

"You've put a lot of work into this Lorina, it's amazing!"

A loud peal of laughter made them both jump. It was the manager guy, the one with the suit and the tablet, a man who had been, to borrow a word from Merida, condescending to Lorina.

"Roy," said Lorina.

"I see Lorina's been hiding her gin in plain sight again!" He reached over to the 'drink me' bottle, unscrewed the lid and sniffed. He made a pretend appreciative noise and put the bottle to his lips. "Ooh, glug, glug. It's the good stuff. You really shouldn't keep it to yourself!"

It was appalling behaviour. Couldn't he see that Lorina had put a lot of time and effort into the display? Penny wondered if he'd been drinking, but with only fruit juice on offer, it seemed unlikely.

"Let's get this bloody thing over with," he said and, with much arm waving, herded them unwillingly back towards the drinks.

7

It occurred to Penny that there were pathetically few guests here for Lorina's official farewell. There was the other librarian, Annalise. There was Annalise's mother, Pam, and her daughter, Merida. There was unpleasant Roy. And there was Stuart Dinktrout, leaning against a bookcase with a couple of books in his hand as though he was really here as a library visitor – 'service user', she reminded herself – but just happened to be passing by this little event.

"Right, right, gather round!" said Roy loudly. "There's a formality to these things and the sooner it's done, the sooner we can be home." He grabbed a glass of fruit juice. "Lorina has been with Suffolk library service since the dawn of time."

"Nineteen eighty-two," interrupted Lorina.

"She's put in her time and seen the vital world and work of the library service transformed. From the godawful ticket system to computerised lending to the cloud-based services we provide today. It's out with the old and in with the newer, sleeker models."

Penny didn't think for an instant that anyone had failed to notice Roy's gaze land possessively on Annalise the librarian at that moment.

"Time is served and now it's time for good old Lorina to be put out to pasture. To Lorina!"

He raised his glass high. There were a few confused "To Lorina"s and those who had glasses, raised them.

If that was the kind of farewell Lorina was going to get, Penny could see why she'd want to leave.

"Speech!" said Penny, blurting it out in such a manner that she surprised herself.

"Yes! Speech!" echoed Stuart.

This didn't appear to please Roy, but Lorina stepped forward, clearly prepared to say something. She looked at Roy, glaring at the man until he moved aside.

"Thank you," she said. "This is very much appreciated. To see friends old" — she looked to Stuart, then Pam — "and new" — she looked at Penny. "And Roy too, I suppose," she added.

This drew a little titter from some quarters.

"I have been here for what seems like forever," said Lorina. "And although this is my last official day, I will be hanging around until World Book Day next week when I will be showcasing one of Penny's creations."

Penny gulped. A creation? One of *her* creations? Oh, if Lorina only knew how little Penny understood about dressmaking!

"Working here has been such a strange adventure,"

Lorina continued. "Dealing with the most wonderful and unusual customers. The little coded notes naughty readers put in books to remind themselves which ones they'd read. Finding rashers of bacon left between pages, as bookmarks. And not only that. Leaves. Cinema tickets. Unposted letters left in a copy of *Adrian Mole*, which we helpfully posted, of course. Chequebooks returned to their owners. I am glad to have been part of the community service that libraries provide, even in this internet age. The people who we've helped apply for jobs and for benefits. The family trees we've researched. The little lies people thought lost to history. I've loved every moment of it."

She looked about, sweeping her gaze across all of them. There might have been a frown as she looked at little Merida, which was odd, but she managed a smile at most of them.

"Yes, thank you," she said, and raised her glass of fruit juice.

"I don't think we need to drink this rubbish," said Stuart and, from behind his back, he produced a bottle of fizz.

Lorina laughed. "Veuve Cliquot rosé!"

"Your favourite!"

Pam stared at Stuart in stunned surprise. Penny thought it was perhaps unusual to bring alcohol into a library, but this was a retirement party, after all. Stuart had the foil off in seconds, and there swiftly followed the pop of a cork. Drink splashed on the floor.

"Mind the books!" said Annalise. "Let me..."

She took the bottle from laughing Stuart and carefully carried it into the kitchen office space to the side. Pam followed her, trying to catch droplets as she went.

Lorina winked at Stuart. "Trying to get into my good books?" she said.

"If you could only point me in the direction of any good books," he replied.

Roy leaned against a display and looked at Penny.

"I saw you in here earlier, didn't I?" he asked.

"Yes," replied Penny and smiled politely, "a service user."

"Good to see all sorts invited. It's one of the metrics I'm measured on, you know, inclusion and diversity. A box ticked is always good news."

"Happy to help," said Penny. "Have you always been a people person, Roy?"

"Very much so!" smiled Roy. "Natural leader of men."

Penny was astounded at the thickness of the man's skin. "Thank goodness! The women do their own thing then, do they?"

Roy stared at her for a moment, then barked out a short laugh. "Very good, very funny! Men means mankind, though. Obviously."

"Does it always mean that, though?" Penny asked.

"Yes, it does. To educated people, anyway."

Someone had found some music, and light pop played from wall speakers.

"People educated with the wording of the Equality Act, you mean? I'd have thought a library manager would be aware of that, at least."

Penny watched as Roy's face turned a deep plum colour. She wasn't certain if it was anger or embarrassment that he'd been called out for his casual sexism. She wondered if she should feel bad for the trap but decided that no, she should not.

"Now listen, young lady, I don't know if you think you're being clever, but that sort of insinuation is uncalled for!" he hissed. "And it's library service area manager!"

Penny put a hand on Roy's arm. "Lovely to see you again, Roy, but I really must go and get a glass of fizz."

Penny left the library service area manager scowling and went over to Lorina. Pam was emerging from the kitchen with a plastic tray of drinks. Annalise was following, swiftly dropping drinking straws into each, much to her mum's irritation.

"No, no, I'm struggling to carry them as it is."

Penny felt Roy's presence at her shoulder. "I'm not a sexist, you know," he hissed.

"Is that so?"

There was some argument about whether champagne, rosé or not, should be served with drinking straws. Lorina took one of the glasses for herself. Roy, taking his cue from this, picked up two glasses and gave one to Penny.

"I *love* women," he said in a very earnest tone. "And I do mean that in two ways."

Lorina slipped over, sipping her celebratory drink through a straw.

"I hope Roy is not being a pest," she said.

"He was just telling me he loves women in two ways."

"Only two?" said Lorina.

"What I meant —" Roy began but Lorina cut him off.

"Just drop dead, Roy. This is my party."

And that was him told. Roy slunk off. Lorina smirked at him in satisfaction before turning back to Penny.

"Now, do tell, have you started work on my dress yet? Blue is absolutely my favourite colour," she said, twirling her blue drinking straw.

"Ah, well," Penny began. "We're just in the early stages..."

8

Penny returned to Cozy Crafts as evening settled over the market town.

Shopkeepers were closing up for the day, and the lights above the hanging baskets outside the Crown Hotel were casting a yellow glow. A man sat with his dog by the old stone cross at the centre of the marketplace, seemingly content to watch the town pack its wares away for the day.

Penny entered the shop, thinking only then that she would need to get a key for herself.

"Who is it?" shouted Izzy from upstairs.

"Burglars!" Penny shouted back.

A few moments later, Izzy descended the stairs with what appeared to be a rolling pin raised high in her hands.

"You actually thought I might be a burglar?" said Penny.

"You said."

"What kind of burglar announces themselves?"

Izzy thought. "An honest one?" She thought some more. "Or a clever one. One who thinks that if they tell everyone they're a burglar, then everyone will assume they're joking and that they're not a burglar. It'd be clever, that."

"I'm not a burglar."

"I can see that now. Come upstairs. I'm just making the cocoa."

"Cocoa?"

"Yes. It's a chocolatey drink. I'm surprised you've not heard of it."

"I was expressing surprise, not ignorance," said Penny, following her up the stairs. "Cocoa sounds... lovely."

"Go straight up to your room. I'll bring the drinks. How was your evening?"

"It was odd and weird and uncomfortable," said Penny. "And sweet too, I suppose. I met the other librarian. And her mother and her daughter. And Stuart Dinktrout, the garden centre owner. And I bumped into the library boss manager person again, an obnoxious little —"

Penny stopped and stared. She had followed Izzy up to the first floor and then continued past her to the top floor, raising her voice so she could be heard by Izzy below, but her words dried up completely at the sight of her room.

Izzy had worked wonders in Penny's absence!

The room was cleared. The bed, with its black iron bedstead that suggested creaking iron springs beneath, was now covered in plumped up white bedsheets and pillows. Izzy had also cleared away space to reveal two high-backed armchairs by the windows and even a little table. It was true that much of the rest of the space was still taken up with fabric, and the landing outside was lined with bolts of cloth like soldiers on guard, but in here, Izzy had uncovered a lovely room that Penny could very much call home.

"Sorry," said Izzy, coming up the stairs behind her. "You seemed to stop talking there like you'd been surprised by the lovely little bedroom you found."

Izzy was carrying a tray on which there were two large steaming mugs of cocoa and a plate of biscuits. She put the tray on the table between the two chairs.

"Which chair?"

Penny plumped for the taller green chair, which left Izzy with the wider purple chair. Both were well padded and very comfortable. Penny looked at the biscuits. There was quite a selection, including party rings, pink wafers and Garibaldis.

"You didn't find those biscuits in here?" asked Penny, afraid of how old they might be.

"Reduced selection box at the Co-op. Picked them while looking for snacks for the newspaper editorial meeting later." She glanced at the clock on the wall. "Thirty minutes for cocoa and biccies, then I'm off over there. Did you say you met Stuart Dinktrout?"

"I did," replied Penny, selecting a shortbread biscuit to dip into her cocoa. "Seemed nice enough, although he was really quite rude about his Arabella."

"Oh!" said Izzy, opting for a custard cream. "Everyone thinks she's lovely. I've been asked to make a waistcoat for her and do a picture feature."

"Stuart was quite unpleasantly scathing about her appetites. He said she was an absolute pig."

Izzy laughed. "Well, of course she is. Everyone knows that."

Penny pulled back. "Oh, so he's not alone in that opinion, then?"

"It's not opinion. It's fact."

"We all have our struggles, with weight or other habits. If Arabella happens to be a bigger eater or something then there's no need to —"

Izzy reached over and put a hand on Penny's knee. "No. She is a pig."

"Izzy…"

"Four legs. Curly tail. Oink, oink."

"What?"

"She lives in the petting zoo bit of Dinktrout Nurseries. Very popular. A sort of mascot."

Penny was silent as she re-evaluated her conversation with Stuart Dinktrout. "Oh. Oh, right." She frowned. "Hang on. Did you say you were going to make her a waistcoat?"

"Yes. This all came about because of a regular feature in the newspaper," said Izzy. "Animal Corner. It started off with pictures that I took around the place of animals that I spotted. Then people started sending me their own pictures of their pets and livestock."

"You are a significant contributor to this newspaper, then?"

"Of course," replied Izzy proudly. "Writing it. Spot of editing. Even delivering it. Anyways, I got a lot of animal features going on. I'm sure Arabella the pig will be popular. But the reader favourite at the moment is a Border Collie called Star, and I've been running more and more pictures of her. People love them."

"It sounds adorable," said Penny.

"Oh it is," said Izzy. "The thing is, though, Star is a smart dog and there are pictures of her doing all sorts of things. She does dog agility trials, she herds ducks and she wears hats sometimes. I think Arabella is a bit more limited, so we've been asked to make her a waistcoat to get her in some more exciting pictures."

"Hang on," Penny said. "I'm still processing the idea of the collie dog herding ducks and wearing hats."

Izzy smiled. "I'll dig out some back issues. You'll love it."

Memories of childhood summers were coming back to Penny. Izzy would immediately try to draw Penny into her latest scheme, no matter what else was happening. They would turn up home, hours late for their meal because the den just *had* to be built and furnished. Izzy had turned into a woman equally passionate about her crazy projects, and not just those related to fabrics and sewing.

Penny sipped her cocoa. It was velvety, warm and coated her throat all the way down.

"So this waistcoat. Break it down for me, Izzy. If you were making a waistcoat for a human, how would you measure them?"

"Pretty easy stuff," Izzy told her. "I'd measure their chest, and maybe their waist if they had a bit of a tummy. I'd also take a back measurement to see how long it needed to be. I just need to do the same for Arabella. Somehow."

There was a twinkle in Izzy's eye, as though she could already see the pig in its waistcoated glory.

"The obvious material to use is brocade. Heavy but very decorative. Although I could have some fun with a patterned quilting cotton. A bit whimsical, although it would require interlining to make it sturdier. I'll pop over tomorrow to do the measuring if you think you can look after my shop for an hour or two."

The mention of 'my shop' had not gone unnoticed by Penny. It had been a crazy, rushed and confusing day, and the pair of them had not yet established a working relationship, a hierarchy.

Izzy drank her own cocoa and nodded out the window.

"Old McGillicuddy with his Timmy by the market cross again." The old man and his equally old dog were indeed still sat out there in the dusk, watching the world go by. "Twice a day, they're out there. Timmy just wants to come to the market and sit. Not one for the exercise, and I reckon McGillicuddy just indulges him."

The dog did indeed look tired and grey.

"And how old is Timmy?" asked Penny.

Izzy sucked her breath in. "Seventy. Seventy-five."

"The dog is seventy-five years old? No. That can't be right."

Izzy scowled at her. "Timmy's the man." She drained the last of her cocoa. "Do you often mistake animals for people, Penny?"

"I..."

Izzy smiled slyly. "Reckon I'm going to have to keep an eye on you. Right, off to the meeting!"

9

Izzy made it to the editorial meeting of the Frambeat Gazette with minutes to spare.

The Gazette didn't have its own building, so the meeting took place in the community room at Miller Fields sheltered accommodation on Fore Street, where Nanna Lem had lived until recently and where the Gazette's editor-in-chief happened to live.

There was a long-standing agreement that replenishing the communal biscuit tin was adequate compensation for the use of the space. It was a large rectangular room furnished with comfy chairs. They were a specific kind of comfy, Izzy had always thought, very much a granny-chic look, with old-fashioned styles and seats that were easy to get up from. There were a great many plants in the room as well, all very carefully tended and arranged in pleasing clusters. There were tables between clusters of seats, so that there was always somewhere to put down a cup of tea. A serving hatch led onto a kitchen area where drinks flowed continually, as anyone who put the kettle on would automatically provide refills for anyone else who wanted one. Izzy had heard people say that they would never live in a place like Miller Fields, but she found it difficult to see any downsides — the slice of life that she observed seemed idyllic.

They sometimes shared the space with other interest groups. Nobody minded if it was board games or the book group, but they all kept a wary eye out for the occasional one-off special. There had been one memorable occasion, several years ago, when guinea pigs had been brought in for something called Small Pet Therapy. The editorial notes had disappeared off a chair while they all sampled some new biscuits, and before anyone had noticed, every scrap of paper had been eaten. It had made no significant difference to that week's Gazette, but it was still mentioned in hushed tones as the 'GP incident'. Izzy had never understood the need for coyness. It made it sound much worse than it really was. Perhaps that was the point.

The editorial meeting was supposed to be where the creative power of the Gazette's contributors combined to make each issue a resounding success. What most often happened was closer to a bewildered post-mortem on the problems that had arisen from the previous issue.

The editor in chief was an elderly ex-military Jamaican gentleman named Glenmore Wilson. Glenmore had lost his left arm some years before. No one knew or dared ask if it had been lost in military action. Glenmore loved the Gazette dearly and had a vision for each issue that inspired and delighted them all. He would direct the content, talk about the themes, and size each contribution in such detail that everyone was certain it was going to be a stunning success. Izzy suspected that Glenmore suffered from some rare and undiagnosed eye condition, though, because the gap between Glenmore's vision and the actual execution tended to be vast.

"We have *never* stipulated how large the typeface should be for our small ads," said Glenmore. "The expectation should be clear from the title. Small ads are *small*. If I need to adjust them to make space then I'm well within my rights."

"Um, yes, Glenmore. We do understand your point, but there is also an expectation that our readers should be able to *read* the small ads. These are too small." This comment came from Tariq, the student. Every so often, a university student would join the Gazette as part of the work experience they needed for their degree course. They brought with them fresh ideas and high standards of technical ability, but invariably they lacked the skills to persuade Glenmore to change his ways.

"I can read them perfectly well!" Glenmore wielded a magnifying glass that was attached to a chain around his neck. He stared around at the rest of the team, defying anyone to argue.

Annalise was the sub-editor. She fielded requests, received complaints and managed adverts. Annalise worked at the library and, Izzy thought, had probably been at the drinks with Penny earlier. Annalise brought her own strict views on spelling and sentence construction, but her most valued role was being able to manage the balance between the characters in the group in a way that nobody else could.

"I was looking at some grant funding, Glenmore, dear. Did you know that we might qualify for more grants if we document our inclusivity policy? Stuff like minimum font size for the ads and such, so that the hard of sight can read them. It might be worth us looking into that."

"Goodness me, Annalise. Well, yes. Do you mean we just need to write a policy?"

"We need to write it down and then we need to make sure we stick to it. Nothing too troublesome for a man of your talents, I shouldn't think."

"Let's put that on the to-do list then, shall we? If you can work on the policy, Annalise, we'll review it next time."

Everyone present, with the possible exception of Tariq, knew that no policy would be written and nothing would change. Advertisers knew that an advert in the Gazette was a tiny tax on doing business in the town and that they were really just paying to keep the eccentric publication afloat.

Izzy met Tariq's gaze and gave him a small smile. Maybe there was useful training to be had here after all, although it wasn't necessarily in journalism.

"Now," Glenmore turned to Izzy. "Tell us about this pig story you're working on."

10

Izzy cycled over to Cozy Crafts bright and early the next morning, only stopping to pick up a couple of items from a café on Market Hill. She went to unlock the shop and found it already unlocked. Penny was inside and behind the counter.

Izzy was excited to see Penny. It had been years since they had spent any real time together. Penny was looking curiously at the antique till.

"No card machine?"

Izzy shook her head. Penny was clearly very wound up about the dull practical stuff. She needed a little more magic and creativity in her life. Why would you care about tills and contactless card machines when you had a pig to measure up for a waistcoat?

"Sleep well?" said Izzy.

"I crawled into bed as soon as you'd gone. Creaking bedsprings or not, I had the best night's sleep."

"Coffee and a bacon roll all right?" asked Izzy, offering a paper bag.

"Very much so. I think you might be right about linen sheets, too. I'm spoiled forever now, I can't go back to boring old cotton!"

"I knew it," said Izzy. She waggled a cycle helmet at Penny. "Have we got time to sort through more of those fabrics upstairs? We might find something suitable for Arabella's waistcoat."

Penny looked at the shop door, perhaps contemplating the likelihood that there might be some early morning customers, perhaps considering the possibility of escape.

"I think we have time," she said.

Over coffee and bacon rolls they continued to look over the stock they'd pulled out of what was now Penny's bedroom. Izzy couldn't help but be distracted by some of the items they uncovered. There was a metal trunk filled with magazines from the fifties, sixties and seventies. Penny cruelly closed the lid and shoved it away in a corner to stop Izzy casually browsing. But that was okay. Izzy had found something else.

"Hey, check this out."

"What on earth is that?" said Penny. "It's like a hacksaw and an umbrella stand had an evil baby!"

Izzy laughed. "The ends are a bit sharp, so take care. It's to store velvet. The thing with velvet, especially the vintage stuff, is that the pile can get crushed. You don't want flattened bits and you don't want fold marks, so the fabric gets hooked onto these spiky bits at each end as it's coiled round in a spiral. It means it's stretched out and doesn't squash the stuff underneath. Like tenterhooks."

"Vintage, huh?" Penny said. "It's certainly got an old-style label. What do you mean about tenterhooks?"

"You know the saying that someone's on tenterhooks, when they are strung out or anxious? Do you know where that comes from?"

"Um, no?"

"Oh, Penny!" Izzy clapped her hands. "You're going to love my 'Word Nerd Corner' column in the local newspaper. It's full of gems like this. When they used to weave fabric from wool centuries ago, it had to be cleaned and then stretched out to dry so that it didn't shrink. The thing that they stretched it out on was a big frame called a tenter. The tenterhooks were like these ones here on this roll, and they held it in place on the tenter." Izzy jabbed a finger on one of the barbs for emphasis.

Coffees done, Izzy cleared the cups away. Lots of good usable fabrics had emerged from their efforts. The job of clearing out all the old stock was only half done, but Izzy had found a dazzling purple brocade fabric that she thought might make a lovely waistcoat for a certain pampered porky.

Coming downstairs into the shop proper, she said, "I was going to go up to Dinktrout's to measure Arabella if you can cope here without me for a couple of hours."

Penny looked around the empty shop as if to indicate that she was unlikely to be swept off her feet by customers. She frowned. Izzy turned to look. Penny had spotted Lem's little sign. It was tacked with a pin to the upright beam of one of the shelves. It was a simple hand-written sheet executed in bright felt tip.

"*Justifiable reasons for murdering customers?*" Penny read.

"Nanna Lem put that up."

Penny looked at some items on Lem's murder list.

"*Using fabric scissors to cut paper. Wasting fabric. Not knowing that knitting is different to crochet.*" Penny unpinned it carefully from the wall. "I don't think we want anything in here that suggests, however jokily, that we want to kill customers."

"If you say so," said Izzy. "I'll be back before lunch with some piggy measurements."

11

Izzy left Penny in charge of the shop and set out for the Dinktrout place. It wasn't very far, and she enjoyed the opportunity to ride her bike, as it was an eye-catching piece of art as well as a mode of transport. She had wrapped multi-coloured yarn around the main tubular steel parts of the frame. Someone had once asked her if she had knitted her own bike, and she still wasn't sure if they'd been joking or not. She had added some storage by making side panniers from colourful oilcloth. They were capacious and beautiful, with a vibrant paisley pattern that always made her smile. For this job she only really needed a tape measure, a pencil and some paper, but she had also popped her wellies in for good measure. She wasn't sure whether the pig pen would be very muddy.

She cycled up the curve of Double Street, lined by crowded, higgledy-piggledy painted houses, and was mildly surprised to see an ambulance and police car parked outside a house which had been painted a startling birthday-cake-icing shade of pink. Izzy nodded at the police officer outside the house and cycled on.

Dinktrout's Nurseries, a mile out of town on the Badingham Road, was one of the largest businesses in the area and seemed to be continually expanding. Izzy had heard of the petting zoo, but had never visited it. She walked through the main shopping area. Like so many garden centres these days, very little of the place seemed to be given over to actual gardening. There were certainly lots of things to put in gardens. There were pottery rabbits and hedgehogs. There were various benches and picnic tables. There was even a selection of tall metal sculptures formed from welded steel for the garden owner who felt their home would be enhanced by a giant metal giraffe, or a deer, or a flamingo.

And then there was the stuff that had very little to do with gardening or gardens at all. There were jigsaw puzzles, glossy books, candles, clocks, mugs, board games, and a selection of bath products the variety of which Izzy found quite remarkable. She took the time to stop and look at the small craft section, and her eyes lingered on a pair of sturdy pink-handled fabric shears that she momentarily coveted before reminding herself that Cozy Crafts was meant to be the place for buying dressmaking accoutrements, not Dinktrout's.

Izzy saw a sign.

CHILDREN'S PETTING *area*

.   .   .

THERE WAS a young woman in wellies standing by the entrance.

"Hi, I'm here to measure up the pig for its waistcoat."

The woman pursed her lips. "Very good. You will need to be more careful with your language, though."

Izzy thought back over the words she'd used. There were no swears, were there? No accidental insults? "Sorry, what do you mean?"

"Arabella is very much a 'she', not an 'it'. You will also find that those who know and love her do not talk about her as a pig. She is very much her own character. You will understand once you've met her."

"Oh. Right. I can't wait."

Izzy followed the woman through the gate. The petting area had a charming farmyard feel. There was a large barn with some goats behind a metal fence. Bales of straw had been placed for smaller children to stand on and feed them from the tubs of food available for purchase. Izzy could see a field with alpacas further away up a path, and there was much excitement in another barn where lamb feeding was taking place.

They walked on into another building, with 'Arabella' painted in huge colourful letters over the entrance. There was no mention of her being a pig, but there were cartoon pictures depicting Arabella as some kind of action hero.

"Arabella only makes appearances at weekends and for the special birthday party packages. I'll need to fetch Mr Dinktrout to open up for you."

Izzy waited for a few minutes. She moved over to look through the large open door of a riding arena. Placid ponies walked round in a large circle with their teenage handlers. Horse people really loved being with horses. Did it all start at a place like this? Izzy wondered whether she would have become a horse person herself if Grandma Lem had owned a pony rather than a sewing shop when Izzy was small. Still, she wouldn't swap her passion for fabrics, haberdashery and sewing machines.

"Ah, you would be the young lady who's come to do the fitting?"

Izzy turned to greet the bronzed silver fox that was Stuart Dinktrout. She knew who he was, of course. He was a well-known businessman, head of the local chamber of commerce, and she had once interviewed him for a local business feature, but his face suggested that he did not remember, so Izzy let it slide.

"I'm Izzy," she said, extending a hand.

He gave her a fond smile and looked at her hand. Izzy recognised that smile. Men of a certain age were bemused by women who wanted to shake hands. Whatever. If he expected her to curtsey or to be seen and not heard then he was going to be disappointed. She kept the hand there, and he gave it a light shake.

"Good. Well, I can introduce you to Arabella. It's one of her rest days of course."

"Of course." Izzy pointed at the cartoons painted on the side of the building. "Can Arabella really play tennis and ride a bike?"

"Not yet. You would be surprised at what Arabella can do, though. I have engaged a tutor."

Izzy didn't know where to begin with that statement. Her

first thought was how on earth did one get a gig as a pig tutor? It sounded both horrific and sort of fun.

Stuart unlocked the door and led the way inside. It was a large open space painted creamy-white. Remembering her wellies, Izzy felt a little foolish: this place was cleaner than most people's houses. There was seating around the edges of the room, for when the children came in. There were cushions and rugs laid in artful arrangements. There was even a television set. There was no pig, though.

"You've got a big place here," said Izzy. "I thought Dinktrout's was just a garden centre."

"Our plant nursery is our core business. My grandfather cultivated the unique and beautiful Dinktrout Rose, key to the family fortune. The petting zoo and our Arabella are just part of the necessary diversification. This is Arabella's main residential space, but those passages lead out to her sun lounge and patio area. She likes to spend time out there as it's adjacent to my own work garden. We spend a lot of quality time together." Stuart smiled and raised his voice. "Arabella! Darling! We're in here!"

Izzy heard a tiny pattering sound in response, and a moment later Arabella appeared from a low tunnel in the far corner. She trotted over to them.

"She's so small!" Izzy was no pig expert, but this creature was much smaller than she had expected. Arabella was the size of a slightly tubby Jack Russell terrier.

"She is a micro pig from a specialist breeder. I cannot of course divulge my source." Stuart tapped his nose, as if to indicate that his pig intel was top secret. "Come on then, my beauty!"

He picked up Arabella and cuddled her in his arms. Arabella looked perfectly at home being cosseted in this way.

"It's lovely that she's happy being handled," said Izzy. "It will make measuring her so much easier."

"She's a dream to work with. Poetry and apples are what you need."

"Excuse me?"

"If you recite poetry to her, she really appreciates it. She is very partial to segments of apple as well. I can let you have a book of poems and some apple pieces to use while you work."

"Thank you," said Izzy.

"Oh, and if you see a rabbit come through here, can you let me know. Percy has escaped from the petting zoo enclosure again."

"Um, I shall do."

12

W hile Izzy was out measuring Arabella the pig, Penny had taken the opportunity to poke around the shop more thoroughly. The fancy dress outfits that were on sale were both cheap and very unlovely. They were also very oddly named, presumably in order to avoid copyright infringement. The shop stocked a selection that included *Where's Stripey Guy?*, *80s Purple Musician Guy*, *Ginger Comb-Over President*, *Pubescent Tortoise Assassin* and *Glasses Wizard Boy*.

She checked labels and packets for the fabric content. There was a great deal of polyester, which she quickly realised was cheap and man-made. The feel of the garments and accessories was something like the filter on a cooker hood — it seemed to do the job, but it wasn't pleasant to touch.

There was a balance, she thought, between selling items that could make the business a quick penny and selling items that brought prestige and kudos. There was little point in Cozy Crafts becoming famous and successful as that place which sold cheap and nasty costumes. Any business had to be commercially successful, but commercialism and consumerism were not the be all and end all of business. She was put in mind suddenly of Lorina's particular distaste for — what did she call it? — Disneyfication. Crass commercialism.

Penny understood the sentiment, although she had no problem with Disney films. In fact, she thought, looking round the less than perfect shop, she wished she could burst into a rendition of "Whistle While You Work" and have a bunch of woodland creatures come in and help her dust and clean the place.

She tried an experimental whistle, and the shop door opened.

"I hear you need help," said a tall young man, entering.

"Blimey," said Penny.

He looked about the place as though he had no idea what kind of shop it was, and then turned to look at Penny.

"Nice solid bones," he said.

It was easily one of the weirdest compliments Penny had ever been given. "Um. What?"

"This building. A lot of places have messed around with their interiors but there's some decent original features here, under the dust."

The man wore scuffed trousers and tough brown work boots. He had big hands, builder's hands. Penny put two and two together swiftly.

"Stuart Dinktrout sent you?" she said. "You're…"

"Aubrey," the man grinned. He had an easy grin, like life was genuinely good and worth smiling at. "He said you needed the woodwork out front painting."

"He did and he was right."

Aubrey nodded some more, like he was constantly tallying things up. "I can get that done for you in no time. I'd have been here earlier, but I couldn't get my van past that ambulance on Double Street. You hear about that?"

"About what?"

"Milkman found someone dead outside their front door first thing this morning. Their own front door, not the milkman's front door."

"Oh, goodness."

"And I hear it's that pink house, which means it's that Roy Cotwin. Mr Dinktrout never shut up about how much he hated the place."

"Roy? From the library?"

"That'd be the one. You know him?"

"Only in passing."

"Not wishing to speak ill of the dead but that might have been the best way to know him," said Aubrey. "I'll go get my gear from the van."

13

I zzy was alone in the large white room with Arabella. She was equipped with a plastic tub that contained neat segments of apple and a book of poetry called *Epic Odes of the Farmyard.*

Izzy put down the apples so that she could flick through the poems, as she wasn't sure what kind of epic odes a farmyard might have to offer.

"Here you go, Arabella. Let's read a line for you. *And thusly did the chicken say: I'm sorry pig, I'll mend my ways.*"

Izzy puffed out her cheeks. She wasn't sure that she wanted to read more of this stuff, particularly since the poet clearly had a loose grip on the term 'epic'. She'd rely on the apples instead. She reached down to get her tape measure and saw that the plastic tub was empty. She hadn't even seen Arabella move, but somehow the little pig had snaffled all of the apple slices. "Good grief Arabella, that was sneaky."

There was a small snorting noise that sounded suspiciously like piggy laughter.

"I see we're going to have to resort to poetry. I can't say I'm a fan of these farmyard odes. I wonder if they were written by your owner, eh?" Izzy gave the tape measure a thoughtful tug between her hands. "Let me think of something better."

Arabella gazed up at Izzy, an intelligent look, full of expectation.

"There was a young piggy called, er, Belle," started Izzy, thinking on her feet. She carefully wrapped the tape measure around Arabella's chest while she searched for a second line. "Who exuded a very nice smell." It was true. Arabella had been bathed in shampoo that smelled of vanilla. "She was dainty throughout, from her tail to her snout, and was clearly a brainbox as well!"

Izzy was pleased with her effort, but she was nowhere near as pleased as Arabella was. The little pig ran in circles, squealing with delight.

"Did you really understand that?" said Izzy in amazement. "Right, well if you let me complete my measurements, I'll say it again, how about that?"

Arabella sat to attention ready for Izzy to take more measurements.

In a few short minutes, the measurements were done, and Izzy was even able to get a few simple sketches down in her notebook. She took a few photos on her phone — who didn't want some snaps of a winsome pig? — and then left Arabella to it.

Stuart Dinktrout had mentioned that his own work garden was near here. It wouldn't be a bad idea for Izzy to go over and discuss fabrics with him. Although she was making this garment for free for a newspaper feature, there might be other opportunities to be had. If there was an opening for a paid personal designer to Dinktrout's pampered porker, there would be nobody better suited for the role than Izzy. She crossed Arabella's patio area and, from across a short fence, thought she could hear Stuart's voice.

She approached the fence, peered about politely, and then stepped over into a small, walled rose garden. The roses here were a striking and unusual type, white petals with deeply red edges. To a certain extent, they reminded Izzy of the symbolic Tudor rose, but these blooms seemed almost as though someone had taken a tin of red paint to the edges of white roses.

She walked through the garden and the rich scent of the roses. A little further along was a garden office, its double doors open wide. She stepped inside, expecting to find Stuart here. There was a desk and a computer. There was a folder of paperwork and a stack of books that, on brief inspection, revealed themselves to be a collection of local history books, many of them the popular self-published sort with photos of yesteryear inside, many with coloured strips around their spines that suggested they were from the town library.

But there was no Stuart here. The voice was coming from round the office and further down the path.

"— that's what I hear, anyway," said Stuart. "My friend at the hospital says it looks like classic poisoning. The stupid beggar ingested something. Dead before he got his key in the door. Point is, I want to get onto the solicitor ASAP. If they'll permit us we can have that eyesore repainted a respectable white or Suffolk pink before the weekend. It's a stain on the character of the town. Yes."

Stuart was standing at the end of a path between planted borders. Beyond him were the nursery greenhouses. The air was heavy with the smell of plant life, of flower scent and fertiliser. Stuart turned, mobile phone to his ear. He was neither surprised nor annoyed to see Izzy approaching him through his own private corner of the nursery grounds.

He waved at her casually, said his goodbyes to the person on the phone and put it away.

"Got a little lost?"

Izzy looked back the way she'd come.

"I hope Arabella gave you all you needed," he said. "My darling little duchess, she is."

"Nothing but a delight," Izzy assured him.

14

Penny was interested to spend more time in the shop, and see who came through the door. She was looking forward to some bustling retail activity to take her mind off the sudden death of a man only two streets away. Unfortunately, though, things were neither bustling or active in Cozy Crafts; to Penny's dismay, only one person called in during the course of the morning, and she wanted to buy a single reel of cotton. No amount of helpful fussing around the woman would make that cotton reel magically earn more than a few pennies. It occurred to Penny only then that she hadn't even discussed a salary with Nanna Lem. Sure, it was handy living rent free upstairs, and she supposed Nanna Lem would have the funds to cover the utility bills, but Penny had some personal expenses, too, and she supposed she might need to actually eat before Nanna Lem was well enough to take over again.

Penny went to the kitchen area on the first floor to

investigate the situation regarding food and drink supplies. There were the makings of tea, coffee and cocoa to be found. There was a veritable mountain of half-consumed packets of biscuits: Rich tea, digestive, hobnobs, malted milk, bourbon, gingernuts, crunch creams. There were four and half packets of Nice biscuits. There was also a tub of sugar. Someone had been incautious with the teaspoon over the years. There were tea and coffee stains in the sugar and much of it had melted and reset into a solid lump.

There were no other foodstuffs there, and perhaps Penny shouldn't have expected otherwise. Unless she wanted to live off a diabetes-inducing diet of sweet drinks and biscuits, she'd have to get the shop to make some actual money.

As she turned from the kitchenette, she saw a face looking in at her through the landing window. She gave a yell of surprise. Aubrey the painter gave a shout of alarm in response. Penny thrust up the sash window, her heart still thumping with shock.

"What are you doing?" she snapped.

"Er, cleaning up the windows for repainting." He held up a scraper and a cloth in evidence as he shifted on his ladder.

"I thought you were doing downstairs first."

"Quick worker," he said. "Didn't mean to startle you. Sorry."

She relented at once, and looked back at the kitchen.

"Can I make you a cup of tea?" she asked.

"That'd be lovely. You got soya milk?"

"I can get some," she said, smiling wryly.

He caught her smile and smiled back. "Thought I wasn't the sort to want non-dairy in my tea?"

"Maybe."

"Bet you thought I didn't look like an Aubrey, neither," he said.

"I wouldn't know what an Aubrey would look like," she conceded.

"Quite. Means 'king of the fairies', so you can imagine how well that went down at school," he grinned.

She shut the window, boiled the kettle and, confirming her suspicions that Nanna Lem's supplies wouldn't stretch to soya milk, went out to the little supermarket to pick some up.

Standing outside the shop a few minutes later, with a non-dairy tea for Aubrey and a regular tea for herself, she could see he had already finished the entire shop facias, bar the door and surrounds. He was up his ladder, cleaning the paintwork around the first floor windows.

"Got your tea here," she announced, careful not to startle him into falling.

"Lovely," he said. "You given any thought to the shop sign?"

The name of the shop had been barely readable when Penny had come to the town. Now it was obliterated by the new glistening paint.

"Will you be able to paint me a new one?" she asked.

"Stuart didn't tell me that was part of the job," he said as he scraped off flakes of loose paint. "Then again, he didn't tell me it wasn't, either. Reckon I could do you a nice new shop name once this paint's dried."

"Thank you."

He shrugged atop his ladder. "The sun is shining. It's great working out. I get paid whatever I do."

Izzy parked up her bicycle next to the shop and joined Penny. She looked up too.

"You been standing here staring at builder's bums all morning?" she asked.

"I have not," said Penny.

Izzy took a cup of tea from Penny's hand.

"That's Aubrey's. It's got soya in it," said Penny.

"Oh," said Izzy, swapping one for the other. "This must be mine then."

Penny smiled, resigned to making herself a fresh cup of tea. "How did it go with Arabella?"

"She's such a sweetie," said Izzy. "An apple or two and she loves you forever. I did a picture, look." She passed the paper over to Penny. "I'm practising the style used in fashion sketching."

"What does that mean, exactly?"

"Mostly it's about the use of altered proportions, so everything shows the garment in its best possible light."

"Is that why Arabella looks like a greyhound dressed up by Beatrix Potter?" asked Penny with a laugh. "I bet she doesn't really look like that!"

"No, I jotted her vital statistics just below the sketch, she's a fine full-bodied figure of a pig."

"Good. Of course, we're not actually getting paid for this project, are we?"

"Best get started on that Alice in Wonderland dress for the library lady, then."

Izzy strolled inside. As Penny made herself a cuppa, Izzy went up to the top floor. After a few minutes there was a victorious "Ah-ha!", and she came back down with the fine if slightly elderly white pillowcases that she had discovered on Penny's first day.

"These are going to be for Alice's apron," Izzy declared.

"The pinafore dress bit?"

"Yes. Come on, let's make a start."

Penny followed her down to the shop. "But don't we need to make the dress first?" she said.

"I can see why you think that. That's your logical brain, that is. No, we will make the dress afterwards, because it's a little more complex, and fitted. An apron is made from mostly rectangles with lots of straight lines, so it's easy."

Penny picked up the pillowcase and examined the embroidery. "Can we really make it from these?"

Izzy nodded. "We can definitely get the top part from there, and showcase those lovely yellow flowers. For the skirt part of the apron, we can use some fabric off one of the rolls. The yoke part is where we should use the flowers. It will be about the size of this A5 notepad."

The two of them spent a few minutes moving the pillowcases around on top of the notepad. Penny was hesitant at first, but Izzy helped her to examine the positions that showed off the flowers to best effect.

"Here!" she announced at last.

"Yup, I think so," said Izzy. "Add on a seam allowance and we have our first piece."

Izzy found a basic pattern on the internet and chalked out shapes on the pillowcase. As predicted, they were mostly simple rectangles, so they didn't need a paper pattern.

"As long as we arrange things so that those rust spots are

in the waste, or even in the seam allowances, then we're good."

Penny drew her fingers across the fabric. "I think I can definitely feel the difference between cotton and linen now."

Izzy nodded proudly. "Smooth and crisp, yeah? The slight stiffness is why linen clothes are cool to wear in hot weather because they don't cling to the body. Linen fibres are excellent conductors of heat as well, so they remove heat from the body."

"It definitely is a whole load of rectangles," said Penny when they had cut out all of the pieces.

"Yes. It won't always be like this. When we start making garments we need to deal with curves. This will be fun though, because now I shall introduce you to the mysteries of the ruffler."

"Pardon?" Penny said.

15

I zzy began to explain.

"This apron will have gathered ruffles over the top of the shoulders. There's a boring way of making ruffles, and there's an exciting way. Guess which way we'll be doing it?"

"The exciting way?" ventured Penny.

"That's right." Izzy nodded. "We're going to use this little gem."

Izzy went over to the old-fashioned treadle sewing machine and opened a drawer. She pulled out the alleged ruffler and placed it in Penny's hand.

"What on earth is this?" Penny gave the weird contraption a wiggle and found that it moved. "It's like some kid tried to make a robot out of Meccano and got bored after the feet."

"Oh-ho! It is indeed a foot," said Izzy. "It goes in place of the regular presser foot on the machine."

"The what-what?" It was like Izzy was speaking a foreign language. Was this because it was Izzy talking, or was dressmaking full of weird language?

Izzy put the ruffler in place on the treadle machine. "I'll take a piece of scrap and show you ruffler magic!"

Izzy selected a long thin piece of scrap and fed it into the ruffler. It made a rhythmic clunking sound as it rode up and down, crinkling the fabric into neat pleats as it stitched a line along the edge. Izzy continued for a few more inches and pulled it out to show Penny. "What do you think?"

Penny held the sample in her hand. "That was amazing. How can such a wonderful thing as this exist in the world, and I've never seen it before?"

"I know, right? It's like a tiny mechanical marvel. Come on, you have a go. We can put this foot onto one of the electric machines so you don't need to learn to treadle just yet."

Izzy watched with glee as Penny discovered the thrill of making tiny uniform pleats with the impossible-looking gadget. The construction of the apron was very fast, and once it was pressed Penny stood up to model it in front of the ornate full-length mirror that stood between racks.

"This is beautiful! Look at it!" Penny smoothed the fabric down and admired the crisp lines.

"Great job, Penny. We just need to make the dress now."

Penny swished the apron around admiringly. "How much are we going to charge Lorina for this dress?"

"Does the cost of things matter, when we are creating beauty?" asked Izzy, in the tones of a person who thought she was imparting deep wisdom.

"Um, yes," said Penny.

On a shelf below the cash register, Penny had found Nanna Lem's double entry bookkeeping ledgers. Lem had still been using paper accounts while the rest of the world had moved to computers.

"We have to turn a profit," said Penny. She showed Izzy the latest entries in the handwritten ledger. "This is worrying."

"I mean her writing is a bit spidery, it's true," Izzy agreed.

"I don't know how much longer a business like this can survive."

"Lems sounds like that sometimes. She'll get depressed and say we needed to modernise and go on about things like cash webcasting or whatever."

Penny had no idea whether Izzy meant cash forecasting or something else entirely. "So, roughly what percentage of sales is online, as opposed to in the physical shop?"

Izzy paused, her hot tea halfway to her mouth. "Online? As in, on a website?"

"That's how it's usually done."

"We don't do that yet. I did start to build us a website but I got a bit waylaid."

"Waylaid? By what?"

"Choosing a domain name. Would you believe that back when I first looked into it, the domain for fabricabulous dot com was free? Nana Lem didn't want to change the business name to that though, so we hit a bit of an impasse."

"I see. When was this?"

"Oh, about four, five years ago," said Izzy.

"Fabricabulous," said Penny, trying it out. "It doesn't even sound all that nice when you say it. We need to revisit those plans and get some online presence."

"Oh, can we do a mood board?" Izzy jumped up. "I love a mood board! Getting a design colour palette together, too."

"Yes, of course, that would be lovely." Thoughts of colours made her think of the pink house and Aubrey's news. "You'll never guess who was found dead this morning?" she began, but got no further as the door chimed and two women entered.

"Morning!" said Penny, almost yelling the word in her delight at seeing fresh customers.

"It is!" one agreed, mirroring her enthusiasm. "We were looking for costumes for the kids for World Book Day."

"Let me show you what we have over here," said Penny, directing them to the display of ready-made costumes.

"We want Wonder Woman or Moana," said one of the women.

Penny was immediately put in mind of Lorina's grumblings about costumes that were nothing to do with books. She couldn't afford to alienate customers, though, so she smiled and said nothing while the women browsed.

"Can we bring them back and change them if they don't fit?" asked the other woman.

"No," said Izzy.

"Yes," said Penny, at the same time.

The two women exchanged a glance and moved towards the door.

"Sorry for the mixed message," said Penny. "We're trying out a new returns policy. No questions asked if you return within seven days."

They resumed their browsing.

"Smart move," said Izzy in a low voice. "World Book Day is more than seven days away, otherwise you can bet your boots they would dress the kids up in those outfits and bring them back here the day after for a refund."

"We need to generate extra value for these people, to keep them coming back," Penny replied.

"Two costumes each?"

"No. Something that makes people want to come here."

"A workshop, you mean?"

"Maybe..."

"Teach the kids how to make a book tote with their name on?"

Penny turned to Izzy, her eyebrows arched with delight. "What? Yes! That! Seriously, you could do that?"

"Sure."

One of the women held up a pre-packaged costume. "What is *Hungry Rebel Girl*?"

"I think that's the non-copyrighted version of Katniss Everdeen from the Hunger Games. That's from an actual book."

"Oh. I thought it might have been Black Widow."

"No, you need to look for *Ginger Catsuit Assassin*," said Izzy helpfully.

Penny strode over to the women. "Not sure if you might be interested in the World Book Day workshop we're running? It's so new we haven't even made the posters yet. The children will learn how to make a World Book Day book tote with their name on."

"Sounds nice. How much? And when?"

Penny turned to Izzy.

"Fifteen pounds each plus cost of materials?" suggested Izzy. "Do it maybe a week on Saturday?"

"That's after World Book Day," pointed out one of the mothers.

"Have World Book Day and then make a bag to put your books in," said Izzy.

"Not bad," the other mother nodded. "Is that for an hour?"

"No, it will be a three hour workshop," said Izzy.

"Oh brilliant! Yes, mine will come," said the first woman.

"Mine too!"

Penny realised that they had just offered what effectively amounted to bargain-priced childcare. She would need to cost out future workshops more thoroughly with Izzy, but this was a promising start and a way to get cash flowing. "Let me take your details. Pass the word round as well, how many children can we take Izzy?"

"Twelve if they share machines one between two."

Twelve children in that first floor workshop. It would be a challenge. It was another room that they would need to sort out, too.

The women bought a selection of costumes which put less than twenty pounds in the till.

"See you soon!" said Izzy cheerily as they left.

"We have a lot to tidying up to do before the workshop," said Penny. "I'm afraid the mood board might have to wait."

"Not a problem," said Izzy. "Oh, you were going to tell me."

"Tell you what?"

"Who'd been found dead this morning. You were saying."

"That's right. Roy. From the library. Outside his pink house."

"That's sad. He wasn't old."

"Maybe a heart attack, something undiagnosed," said Penny, but Izzy was shaking her head, her eyes suddenly wide.

"Not according to what I've heard," she said. "The doctors think he'd been poisoned."

"How'd you know that?"

"Something I overheard in a rose garden. He'd eaten or drunk something and — ugh!" She stuck out a tongue as though dead. "Very sad. Some people just don't think about what they put in their mouths."

Penny was struck by a sudden and horrible thought. "Oh, God."

She stumbled away from the counter, searching round until she found a cardboard box on the floor. The box of junk she'd brought from upstairs. She pushed aside an ancient mouse trap and turned over one of the dusty and decomposing boxes of rat poison within. She saw the big red triangle and the exclamation mark.

"The bottle was in here," she said.

"What bottle?"

"The 'drink me' bottle. The poison and the bottle and…"

She stumbled forward, almost missed the door and ran out of the shop, heading at full speed for the library.

16

Penny stumbled into the library.

She looked to the counter and gave an awkward nod to the younger librarian, Annalise, before ducking sideways through the non-fiction room, into the corridor and up the wonky stairs that led to the old court room and the Alice display. She feared that the room might be locked, but the upstairs space was open.

There was the Alice in Wonderland display with the old book under the glass case. There were the cakes and the teapot and...

Penny gave a gasp of relief. The bottle was there.

She snatched it up and then felt a sudden revulsion at having touched it. Was this the means by which Roy had died? The bottle had sat for years among the dust and crumbs of ancient rat poison, accumulating a deadly residue.

She looked to the door and replayed the scenes of yesterday in her head.

"Roy comes in. 'Oh, lovely display. Is this your gin stash?' Glug, glug. Ha, ha."

Had his lips actually touched the bottle? She couldn't remember. Should she take this to the police? She certainly shouldn't leave it here. Holding it carefully between thumb and finger as though the poison might leap from it and strike her down, she carried it back downstairs. She realised she couldn't just take it without telling the library, even if it was technically hers.

Pam, Annalise's mother, was by the counter. There was a net shopping bag in her hand, holding a crusty loaf and some fat round oranges.

"Sorry to interrupt," said Penny, leaning round. "I just wanted to say I'm taking this and —"

There was a clatter and an extended grunt of annoyance from somewhere by the children's section, and suddenly Lorina was stomping up to the counter waggling a DVD box of *Thumbelina* in her hands.

She slammed it down on the counter.

"Annalise! What have we said about the Disney thing?"

Annalise looked up at her colleague with patient serenity. "We've said nothing, Lorina. It's mainly you that has all those things to say about Disney."

"It was on the floor! I nearly tripped over it!"

"Hardly a literary criticism, or indeed the fault of Disney. It's a lovely film and a mostly faithful adaptation of the Hans Christian Andersen tale. And technically, it's not a Disney. It was a Don Bluth film."

"I don't care who made it. It's a slippery slope!"

"You're right," Annalise smiled. "One day, a child might

watch that film. The next they might watch *The Little Mermaid* — that *is* Disney. And then they might discover that both stories are by the same author and take out the physical book. I'm sorry you don't approve, but we might want to consider how it's bringing classic stories to a new generation, don't you think?"

Penny couldn't help but silently agree, even if she was surprised that anyone was watching DVDs at all these days. If Annalise was going to be running the library when Lorina was gone, then it was a good thing she was prepared to challenge the status quo.

Annalise smiled at Lorina's final resigned harrumph of displeasure. Was this what happened when you lived in a small town? Did you get weirdly fixated on minor issues? Did you find yourself constantly refighting well-worn battles with your friends and neighbours, taking delight in the most obscure of victories and feeling misery at the slightest defeat?

Lorina's furious eyes turned to the bottle in Penny's hand and then frowned in surprise.

"What are you doing?"

Suddenly, three sets of eyes were on her.

"Oh," she said, as if was surprised to find the bottle there herself. "Um, this is going to seem odd but, you know what happened to Roy..."

"Roy?" said Annalise, and the deeper frown lines around her eyes told Penny that, no, they didn't know. She had assumed that news travelled fast in small towns.

"Oh. Oh, I see. I don't want to be the bearer of bad news and I'm only going on what people have said..."

Pam must have caught Penny's tone, because her hand went to her mouth in shock.

"What is it?" said Lorina.

"He's dead," said Penny. "They found him dead outside his house. Poisoned, they say."

"No," said Annalise.

Pam pinched her lips, dismayed.

Lorina stared. "Poisoned?"

"And I knew this bottle had been stored amongst pesticides... well, I just thought. And he did pick it up and..." She looked to Lorina. "Didn't he?"

"Poisoned how?" said Annalise.

"I think I'm going to be sick," said Pam. She moved awkwardly to the exit. Annalise hurried round to help her mother out into the fresh air.

Lorina held her hand out for the bottle. Penny hesitantly handed it over.

"That bottle was dusty and grimy," said Lorina. "Cobwebs and that. I cleaned it thoroughly. Hot soapy water. A real scrub. I don't think... dead? Like really dead?"

Penny gave her an honest look. "There was an ambulance. The painter guy said it was Roy. Stuart Dinktrout told Izzy that it was poison."

Lorina nodded solemnly. "It does not do well to speak ill of the dead."

"No."

"But it couldn't have happened to a better person."

It was said with such simple, cold matter-of-factness that Penny was stunned.

"Lorina!" she whispered in dismay.

Lorina's look was haughty and Penny had the sudden impression that, while Roy might have been difficult to work with, Lorina was perhaps no angel herself. She leaned in towards Penny, bottle in hands.

"Why do you think that man isn't married or hasn't kept a girlfriend for more than a month? Absolute creep, he is. Was, I should say. Past tense. She won't tell you herself but Annalise has suffered at that man's hands. Literally. Got a life of their own, those hands have. Had." She smiled at her own correction. "Many a woman has suffered with that oily snake brushing up against her in a narrow corridor or placing a 'supportive' hand on her knee during a meeting." Lorina shuddered.

"Did no one report him?" asked Penny.

"I made our displeasure clear to him on many an occasion. Once I even twisted his wrist so hard he couldn't write for a week. But that kind of man..." She looked to the door as though glimpsing his ghost there. "There's no educating a man like that." She jiggled the bottle. "Okay if I put this back in the display? Nothing to worry about here. And I doubt we need to inform the police, eh?"

Penny watched as the woman walked away through the library and then, for want of anything better to do, she returned to the shop. Aubrey was coming down the ladder from the first floor. He wiped his hand on the cloth tucked into his belt.

Penny looked up.

"Wow. What a difference a lick of paint makes," she said, nodding approvingly at the bright and tidy Georgian windows.

"I'll let that dry," he said. "Takes a while this time of year. I'll come back on Saturday to do the sign if it's no trouble."

"If it's no trouble to you," she replied.

His smile was unconscious and natural and all the more attractive for it. It felt like it had been a long time since a man had smiled at her that way.

"I get paid whatever," he said, happily, and started tidying away his things.

Penny went back into the shop.

"He's single," said Izzy, flipping through an aged sewing magazine at the counter.

"Who's single?" asked Penny.

"Huh?" said Izzy looking up.

"Who are you talking about? I didn't ask anything."

"I didn't say anything. You're hearing voices," said Izzy, and went back to her magazine.

17

Penny couldn't help but grin every time she walked past the vintage mannequin. She had found it during her ongoing efforts to empty the room upstairs. It now had pride of place in the shop, and currently displayed the apron they had made for Lorina. The glorious white linen ruffles contrasted nicely with the dark wood of the shelving.

"We can use the mannequin to showcase our wonderful fabrics," said Penny on Friday morning. "Maybe we have a rolling programme of refreshing its outfits."

"Why would we stop at the mannequin?" asked Izzy, with a pointed nod at Penny's jeans and t-shirt.

Izzy was right, of course. "Absolutely! We need to dress ourselves in fabrics so that people can see what they look like. Once we've finished the commission for Lorina, maybe we can make a start?"

"We can and we will," said Izzy firmly. "Now, let me show

you what I think we need for Lorina." She pulled a book from underneath the counter. "This book is a great reference for historical garments."

Penny took the book. *The Cut of Women's Clothes.* She flicked through and saw that it was a textbook featuring line drawings. "Very nice," she said. She didn't want to say anything, but it seemed very old-fashioned in both its style and its layout.

"Don't be fooled by it looking old-school. These patterns are more or less usable," said Izzy, as if reading her mind. "We just have to try and sketch them out at full size."

Penny was sceptical. "They are tiny though!"

"No, look." Izzy flicked through to find a picture that was close to Alice's dress. "This one. See how the tiny diagram has measurements next to it? We get a piece of big paper and, with a little luck and lot of concentration, we can recreate it."

Penny watched as Izzy marked up a scale on a large piece of paper and then laboured over a pencil sketch of the pattern on the page. There was much tutting, huffing and scribbling-out from Izzy.

"Surely there must be a better way?" said Penny. "How about we take a picture of the page and scale it up on the computer?"

"Go on, then."

Penny opened the image editing programme on the old laptop behind the counter that didn't seem to get much use.

"We could overlay a one-inch grid," she said slowly. "And then we just have to make the squares on the grid line up with the markers on the scale."

"Oh," said Izzy. She rummaged under the counter and

produced a sheet of paper with dots and crosses in one inch squares.

It then took less than thirty minutes to draw out the pattern pieces for the dress.

"We can draw on seam allowances and get to work on a toile," said Izzy. "Let's see what sort of size this will be." She pulled a tape measure across the pattern pieces. Penny thought it was perhaps the waist. "Ah yes. I think this is sized for a slender Victorian woman wearing a corset. We'll need quite a few adjustments."

Penny watched as Izzy used pencil, ruler, scissors and Sellotape to chop up and reassemble the pattern in ways that looked unfathomable.

"Nearly there!" Izzy said.

"Does there come a point where it's not even the same pattern?" asked Penny. "You made so many changes to it."

"Everything is up for grabs when we want to make a garment look good," Izzy explained. "We'll make a quick toile and we'll need to change it all again, but at least now I'm confident that it will fit around Lorina's body. Now we cut it out in calico."

Watching Izzy work, Penny realised that she had often done her cousin a disservice. Izzy was a woman of mad and improbable notions. Her dreams and ambitions were wild, her obsessions deep and unfathomable, and her grasp on reality was tenuous at times, but none of that meant that Izzy was useless or incompetent. Penny recalled something she'd once heard, that if you judge a fish by its ability to climb a tree, it will spend its whole life thinking it's stupid. Penny's cousin was that fish and the world was full of trees, but this shop and the art of sewing were the sea in which she swam. Here, amongst the fabrics and threads, Izzy was an absolute genius.

The door jangled and Pam Ockenden entered.

"I saw the poster in the window and — oh, this looks lovely!" She admired the apron on the mannequin.

"It's going to part of a World Book Day costume for Lorina," said Penny. "Part of an Alice in Wonderland dress."

"Ah. Blue, always her favourite colour."

"Seemingly so. Sorry, you mentioned a poster." Penny looked round in case Izzy had put the 'justifiable reasons to murder customers' sheet back up.

Pam pointed at the window where Penny had blu-tacked up a hand-drawn poster.

"A workshop for children. Merida would love to join that."

"It would be great to have her," said Izzy, and picked up the notepad in which she was keeping lists relating to the planned workshop.

"You seem to be a very busy grandma," said Penny.

Pam made a small grunt, neither of annoyance nor agreement. "Annalise's husband is useless when it comes to the childcare. Oh, he works and puts food on the table and such, but if it wasn't for me, Granny Ockenden, I don't know what Annalise would do. It's a strange generation, hers. Yours too, I suppose," she added, eyeing Penny in a manner that made her feel slightly uncomfortable. "I didn't have any help when I was raising Annalise, and I wouldn't have dreamed of asking for it."

"No Granddad Ockenden?" Penny asked automatically, before realising the question might be insensitive.

Pam smiled. There was a tiredness to her smile, as if life was grinding her down and it was hard for the actual smile to break through.

"There's no shame in being a single mother these days, is there?" she said. "It was very different back then. But I had actually come in with another purpose. I wanted to apologise for making an embarrassment of myself yesterday."

"Embarrassment?" It took Penny a moment to realise that Pam was referring to her visible shock at the news of Roy's death. "A perfectly understandable human reaction. A man had died."

"Nonetheless. It's not like we were close."

"I get sad at any death," said Izzy. "I cry when I watch those A&E hospital shows. Even the repeats."

"Lorina was quite, um, dispassionate about the news," said Penny.

"Well, there was no love lost between her and Roy," Pam agreed.

"I hear he wasn't popular with the staff."

Pam grunted again. This one was definitely amusement. "If rumours are to be believed, he practically forced Lorina to take retirement."

"You can't force people to retire," said Penny.

"Not even if they're old and wrinkly?" asked Izzy.

"No."

Pam moved in closer, even though there was quite definitely — sadly — no other customer in the shop to overhear.

"Between you and me, he had a list of complaints against Lorina as long as your arm."

Izzy held out her arm, nodded, and then placed her arm alongside Penny's longer, more slender arm. Penny waved her away.

"Very shirty with the customers sometimes, she is," said Pam. Penny, who had seen and heard Lorina publicly declare her annoyance more than once, found that easy to believe.

"And," said Pam, "there were accusations that she had her hands in the till."

"Do libraries have tills?" asked Izzy.

"They have funds and budgets and a canny individual can divert that money where they wish."

"Well, I never," said Izzy, and Penny saw that Izzy was making other, subtle notes in her notepad. She probably had visions of a front page 'exclusive'.

"But these are all rumours, right?" said Penny pointedly.

Pam shrugged mysteriously. "If it's true, then Lorina wouldn't be the first person to turn to crime to make ends meet. I've been a law-abiding citizen all my life and I haven't got two pennies to rub together." She glanced at the notepad. "This workshop. How much is it?" Before Penny could answer, she had her purse out and was looking in it. "I said I'd help Merida with her school World Book Day costume too. Those things are expensive."

"Depends how creative you're willing to be," said Izzy. "Last Hallowe'en, friend of mine just ran his face through one of those ageing apps, put the photo in a frame and went as The Picture of Dorian Gray."

"Clever," said Pam, not especially impressed.

"Maybe wrap Merida up in toilet paper and send her as the Mummy."

"I don't think that's a book," Penny pointed out, remembering that some people had strong opinions about such things.

"Maybe you've got some old clothes at home that could be repurposed," said Izzy.

Pam laughed. "Spare clothes are not something I have much of. There's an old wedding dress at the back of the wardrobe, but I can't see that being of much use."

Izzy frowned but Penny was struck by an idea. She went out to the cheap and nasty costume section of the shop and found a pack of decorative cobwebs she'd seen there before. She waved them at Pam.

"Wedding dress. Cobwebs. She could go as Miss Havisham from Great Expectations."

"Ooh, that is literary, that," said Izzy.

"Miss Havisham?" asked Pam.

"You know. The old lady who never got married and spends her life bitterly refusing to accept that she's been spurned and sits around in her old wedding dress," Penny explained. "Does the wedding dress have a veil?"

Pam held herself still and quiet for moment. "Don't think it ever did," she said.

"Wait!" said Izzy and dashed off. She returned with a section of cheap tulle cloth from upstairs. A moment with a set of shears, and she had strimmed off enough of the material to make a long veil.

Pam hesitated. "You know, Merida is going to ask me who Miss Havisham is."

"Time to find a decent film version of the book on telly, then," said Izzy.

Pam nodded. Izzy bagged up the veil and cobwebs. Pam looked at her purse again. Maybe times were indeed tight.

"Pay for the workshop and we'll throw these items in for free," Penny told her. The relief on the woman's face was painfully obvious.

"Thank you," she said.

"I thought you were meant to be a hard-nosed businesswoman," Izzy said when Pam had gone.

"I'm a big softy at heart," said Penny. "But don't tell anyone."

18

Saturday morning and the marketplace was buzzing with life. Market stalls filled the cobbles. Vegetables, cheeses, meats and pies were all laid out on wooden trestle stalls. A host of small businesses sold jars of preserves and honey, griddle-cooked street food and freshly baked cakes. Though winter had still not relinquished its grip on the countryside and spring was still definitely around the corner (or indeed the corner after that), it was clear there were tourists in the town, come to enjoy its beautiful centre and perhaps to visit the grand twelfth century castle up on the hill.

Penny spent much of the morning watching the shoppers stroll by, projecting a mental urge for them to come into the shop, but evidently her psychic powers were not very potent. They sold a few cheap costume masks and a little thread, and everyone who did come in commented approvingly on the half-finished Alice dress but, by and large, the crowds ignored them.

Penny had been staring absent-mindedly into the street for so long that it took a while to realise there was someone outside the window, staring right back at her. She blinked. It was Aubrey, the painter. The single painter, as Izzy had helpfully pointed out. He carried a tool box of materials and a ladder. Penny waved him to the door and went to meet him.

"The shop sign?" he began, as a greeting.

"And good day to you," she replied, smiling. "The paint work is marvellous."

"And dried fine," he agreed.

He propped up his ladder and came inside. It turned out he had come well-prepared, with several sheets of paper with possible lettering options for the sign.

"You had a very traditional sign before. Lots of serifs. That's the extra sticky out bits on letters to you and me, but I had wondered if you fancied something a bit cleaner and more modern, like this."

Penny and Izzy looked over the possible fonts.

"I like Comic Sans," said Izzy. "It's such a friendly font."

"You will notice that I haven't brought an example of Comic Sans," Aubrey explained. "It's not generally a good idea unless you're opening a toy shop or children's clothes shop and even then..."

"I like this one," said Penny, putting her finger on a sheet.

"Good choice," said Aubrey. "Helvetica. Clean, clear, easy to read."

"It's not Comic Sans," said Izzy.

"It certainly isn't," agreed Aubrey, pleased. "I'll get right onto it."

"Cup of tea?" asked Penny as he went to the door.

"Thanks. You know how I like it," he said.

When the door swung shut, Izzy slapped Penny's elbow playfully.

"What?" said Penny.

"*You know how I like it.*"

"He was talking about tea."

"That was flirting, that was. I'll get the kettle on and open a packet of nice biscuits."

Soon, Aubrey was up his ladder, sketching out the lettering from the sign. Penny watched him working from the counter. Admittedly, from here, she could only see him from the chest down but that didn't stop her looking.

She regarded the sugar-dusted biscuit she was about to dip in her tea.

"When you said nice biscuits, did you specifically mean these?"

Izzy looked from the old tub of mixed buttons she was sorting through.

"Hmm?"

"You know these are called Nice biscuits."

"Niece, as in my sister's daughter?"

Penny held up the biscuit, displaying the lettering baked into its top.

"Nice, as in the French city."

"But it's spelt nice. Because they are nice biscuits."

"From Nice."

"I don't know where you get your facts from. Anyway, it

doesn't matter; they taste lovely when you put then in your mouth."

Penny found herself musing generally on things put in mouths when she dunked her biscuit one too many times in her tea and the end dropped off.

"If Roy wasn't poisoned by our bottle then I wonder how he did die," she said.

"Oh, is this what we're discussing on a Saturday lunchtime now?" asked Izzy.

She dropped handfuls of teddy bear eyes on the counter in front of Penny. "Sort these into piles of ten, please. I struggle to count when there's all these eyes watching me."

Penny began sorting. "Haven't you wondered what happened?"

"Of course, I have. I think he was murdered," said Izzy.

She said it so in such a plain and straightforward manner that Penny was surprised. "You do?"

"I think it stands to reason. It must be quite hard to accidentally poison yourself. Don't you think so?"

"I agree," said Penny. "I don't think I expected you to think the same."

"Question is, who poisoned him and how?"

"And why aren't the police investigating?"

"They've been up at his house, searching the place. So Glenmore, the Frambeat editor, says."

"Could be suicide," said Penny.

"Not a common method of suicide."

"You know that?"

"I might have googled it. Maybe. I'm admitting nothing. But it seems more likely he was given something earlier that evening which got to work on him by the time he got home."

"He was at the library with me, quaffing expensive champagne at Lorina's leaving drinks."

Izzy wagged a finger at her. "There you go. Poison in the champagne."

Penny separated off another set of ten eyes and Izzy put them in a little plastic bag.

"Plenty of people there who wouldn't have been sad to see Roy out of the picture," said Penny.

"Really?"

Penny shrugged uncomfortably. "Mostly rumours and hearsay. But he was too hands-on with Annalise."

"Hands on?"

Penny did a little gropey hand gesture. Izzy grimaced.

"And Annalise's mum knew that, too," Penny added.

"And there was that business with forcing Lorina to retire over missing library funds," Izzy pointed out.

"Rumours and hearsay and nothing fit for printing in local newspapers," said Penny firmly. "But, yeah, no love lost there."

"Anyone else at the drinks?"

Penny thought. "Apart from a ten-year-old child, there was just me and Stuart Dinktrout."

"Well, he and Roy didn't get on."

"What? The business with the ugly colour of Roy's house? Hardly worth committing murder over."

"You don't know how precious people can be about their town, especially if you're the head of the local chamber of commerce."

"Excluding myself and the child — and the dead man, of course — there were four people at the drinks: Lorina, Annalise, Pam and Stuart."

"Four suspects, then."

Penny considered this and then shook her head. "No, it can't be. Roy had just the one drink, and I saw him drink it."

"So?"

"He picked two drinks off the tray. He gave me one at random and he drank the other. If that glass was poisoned then he passed me a safe one and drank the poisoned one himself."

Penny felt an unexpected chill run through her body.

"Did I... did I nearly drink poison?"

Izzy gave her a sceptical look.

"Who'd want to kill me?" Penny whispered.

"Can't imagine. Do you often criticise the way people pronounce the names of biscuits?"

Penny harrumphed and went outside to offer Aubrey a biscuit.

19

When the packet of biscuits had been entirely polished off and the teddy bear eyes sorted into little bags to sell, Penny decided she would go back to the library and try to visualise whether Izzy's poisoned champagne theory made sense. On the street outside, Aubrey was partway through the lettering job. He had completed 'Cozy' and was just making a start on 'Crafts'.

Penny strolled the short distance down the market hill and down the little cul-de-sac into the library. Lorina sat behind the service desk, sorting out books with a customer. Penny slipped sideways through the non-fiction section, along the corridor and up to the first floor and the old court room. The room was not empty. Children and parents sat around on colourful rugs while Annalise, perched on a box stool, read aloud from a selection of picture books. The children were managing that neat trick of being both attentive and noisy at the same time.

Annalise glanced up momentarily and gave Penny the tiniest smile and wave before returning to the gripping tale of Mole's quest to find his hat on the beach.

Penny looked about the room, trying to cast her mind back to Wednesday afternoon. The possibility that she might have come so close to imbibing the deadly poison still sat like a heavy knot of discomfort in her stomach. She had been standing over there, not far from the Alice in Wonderland display. Lorina had been standing here, doing her little speech, talk of bacon bookmarks and of readers leaving codes in books. She wondered, briefly, what that last one meant.

Then Stuart had brought out the champagne. Yes, it was Stuart who had brought the champagne. If poisoned champagne was the premeditated method for the murder, then Stuart was essential to that plan. He popped the cork, there were bubbles and the rush to get the bottle to the glasses in the kitchen.

Penny stepped back, slipped out into the corridor and opened the door to the little kitchen. It wasn't locked. No one seemed particularly hot on keeping doors locked round here. The kitchen was a reasonably large space with counters and cupboards running along three walls.

"So, they came in here," she mused softly. She couldn't remember who it had been, specifically. Pam and Annalise, was it? Or was it Lorina? She remembered seeing Annalise chasing after her mother and putting straws in glasses, but that was when they were back in the room.

A quick search turned up a lonely cheese sandwich in the fridge, two shelves of glasses in one cupboard, a multi-coloured pack of drinking straws in the cutlery drawer and in the cupboard under the sink, behind a bucket...

"Oh, my," said Penny.

There was a box of rat poison. Inside were sachets, identified on the box as containing granules of rat and mouse killer to be used in poison bait stations only.

"Or glasses of champagne," she whispered.

So that was it. Champagne and rat poison. A sachet poured into a glass and left to dissolve. But that didn't explain how the offending glass had been placed specifically into Roy's hands. Penny didn't touch the box of poison. She didn't want anything to do with it. Perhaps she should tell the police. Obviously, she should tell the police. Shouldn't she?

She backed away slowly and down the crooked staircase, musing over what she should do. She would seem a fool if she simply told the police that the death of a man outside his own house was linked to a box of rat poison in the library kitchen. Roy Cotwin in the library with a box of poison. It sounded like a Cluedo murder.

As she made her way downstairs, she searched the internet for how one might anonymously report crime information, and soon found herself on a *Crimestoppers* website. It seemed an ideal way to report her suspicions, but she stopped when she reached a box that asked her to confirm that her information didn't require urgent police action. It sort of did, didn't it?

Her thoughts were derailed by the sound of a loudly-whispered conversation round the corner in the non-fiction section.

"You may think this is all fun and games, Lorina, but I

don't," hissed a man's voice. Was that Stuart Dinktrout? He sounded angry.

"I think it's the most marvellous fun," Lorina replied.

"If anyone finds out, this could absolutely ruin me."

"I should think so. Don't think I don't know why you've been extra-specially nice to me of late. That thing with the Veuve Cliquot rosé. It was so obvious what you were up to."

"I was trying to be nice to an old friend."

"Less of the old, Stuart. I'm having a perfectly lovely week. Roy is dead and I think we're both happier for it."

"That's callous, Lorina."

"I speak as I find."

"Then since you're in such a happy mood, why not do me the favour of telling me where the picture is."

"All in good time, Stuart."

There was growl of exasperation and the sound of unhappy departure. Penny was frozen with incredulity. Had they been talking about murder? Roy's death? Champagne? Fun and games? Doing each other favours? Had it all been a team effort? Stuart had brought the champagne and Lorina had put the poison in it?

"Oh, what are you doing here?"

Penny nearly choked in surprise as Lorina came into the corridor and saw her.

"Ah. Ah," Penny gasped like a landed fish.

"Did you get lost, perhaps?" asked Lorina, playfully.

Oh, this would not do! To overhear murderers talking and then be cornered by one of them! Penny's mind raced.

"You've caught me out," she said.

"Caught you out?"

Penny pointed up. "I went to the storytime thing upstairs."

"But you have no children."

"No, I, um, thought I might drum up some interest in our children's sewing workshop next Saturday. I know it's not good form to do a hard sell to a captive audience but..."

Lorina laughed. "Oh, what do I care? Sounds lovely! If local businesses are promoting reading, however tangentially." She raised the pile of local history books in her hand, went back into the non-fiction room and began slotting them onto their shelves. "Readers are peculiar beasts. We sometimes have to trick them into reading the good books and curb their naughty ways."

Penny was keen to get away. The feeling that she was alone with a killer was hard to shake off. But she shouldn't raise suspicions. She should keep the conversation going.

"In your leaving speech, you mentioned something about readers leaving coded notes in books. I wondered what you'd meant."

Lorina laughed again. "Let's see. Come."

She went through to the main library room. There were other customers here. Now, no longer alone with a murderous co-conspirator, Penny felt more at ease. Lorina scanned the shelves and selected one.

"Here," she said, pulling a book with a moody-looking cover off the crime fiction shelves. "Some people simply devour crime fiction and often — ha! Here." She showed Penny the title page of the book and, in the bottom right corner, a smudge of green highlighter, a biro'ed star and, in a different pen, the letters 'AH'.

"What is that?" said Penny.

"Readers forget what books they've read, so they mark them with a particular symbol to make sure they don't accidentally take out the same book twice."

"That's quite clever."

"Vandalism, you mean. I have my solutions."

"Oh?"

Lorina beckoned her back to the counter. There was a pile of newly arrived books. Lorina sat down, took the top book and, with a light theatrical manner, marked the early pages with highlighter and biro.

"You mark new books with the readers' own secret marks?"

Lorina beamed. "When they realise their system no longer works, then they'll stop."

"The books are still vandalised."

"Noble sacrifices in the ongoing war to retrain the selfish. Now, in terms of books worth reading…" Lorina reached under the desk and pulled out a wide but thin book entitled *Framlingham's History in Pictures*. "I would recommend you have a read of this."

"Really?"

"A valuable introduction or indeed re-introduction to our historic town."

"I don't have a library card."

And suddenly, like a rabbit produced by a magician, there was a white plastic card in Lorina's hand. "Nothing but the best service for my favourite dressmaker. Any news on when it will be ready?"

"Izzy and I are working on the toile this afternoon so we might be able to do a fitting later."

"Oh, wonderful!"

Penny took book and card in bemusement. "Well, thank you, I guess."

"All part of the service."

Penny stepped outside. Books and library cards and secret codes and whispered conversations. She'd almost forgotten the key point of her visit. There was rat poison and it needed reporting to the police. She wasn't going to call the police directly. That would result in questions and possibly alienating locals, including her first dressmaking client. She went back to the *Crimestoppers* website, found the anonymous tip phone number, and dialled. She moved to the side of the little courtyard to let other library customers go in and waited for someone to pick up.

"Hello, welcome to crime prevention —"

"It's about the death of Roy Cotwin," said Penny swiftly.

"Roy…"

"Roy Cotwin. Framlingham. That's Suffolk. The police know about it. There's rat poison in the library kitchen. That's what killed him."

"If I could just take a few details —"

"Roy Cotwin in the library with the rat poison." God, it did sound like a Cluedo murder. "The police know the details."

And before the woman could ask a further question, Penny hung up.

She forced herself to breathe a sigh of relief that she didn't feel and walked back to the shop.

20

Toiling away with fabric and thread was a good way to ease off the surprises of the day, and Penny threw herself into working on the garment for Lorina. By four o'clock, she had created a toile.

It had taken many hours and a lot of unpicking. Izzy insisted that unpicking and adjusting were skills that were at least as important as construction, but Penny was certain she was just trying to make her feel better. The calico toile was for Lorina to try on for fit, so Penny phoned her to let her know.

As soon as she came through the door, Lorina spotted the apron. "Oh my! Is that for the Alice outfit? It's very good, very authentic!"

Penny smiled with pride. "Yes it is. The dress needs to be more fitted, though, which is why we made a mock-up in calico."

"I'll slip straight into it," said Lorina.

She went to the bathroom to change. Penny watched her come down the staircase, looking critically at the shape of the garment. Izzy walked down to help.

"Hey, that's not bad," said Izzy. "We need to shorten the shoulder seam a little. The waist can come in too." She began to pin the adjustments into place. "I'm using safety pins so that you don't stab yourself when you take it off, Lorina. How does it feel?"

Lorina moved over to the full-length mirror. "It feels good. Calico is a drab colour, but this will be lovely in the blue. I love blue."

"We know. Let's add the apron, so that we can make sure it all works together," said Izzy.

Penny carried the apron over and helped Lorina to put it on over the dress.

"Oh yes, this will be quite marvellous!" Lorina grinned at her reflection. "Very authentic!"

Penny had a brainwave while Lorina was upstairs removing the toile. She pulled out Izzy's copy of *The Cut of Women's Clothes* and put it out on the counter to show Lorina. "I thought you might like to see where the pattern came from."

As Penny had suspected, Lorina was thrilled to see the origin of the dress, in a vintage book. "This is very good. I'm so excited to see that it's directly based upon a period garment as well. What an achievement, well done to the two of you, I can't wait to see the finished thing."

As Lorina left, Penny turned to Izzy, prepared to tell her the tale of her startling visit to the library, but the door opened again instantly and Aubrey walked in, wiping his hands with a cloth.

"Sign's all done," he said. He nodded at the apron Izzy was putting back on the mannequin. "That looks nice."

Penny was seized by an irrational fear that he might reach out and touch it with his paint-smeared hands, even though he'd made no move towards it. Perhaps he'd seen her staring because he looked at his hands and smiled.

"I had wondered if I could just wash my hands in your sink. This one shot paint really clings."

"Yeah, sure," said Penny and pointed to the stairs. "Upstairs and it's... well, it's the room with the sink."

Aubrey went upstairs. Penny dithered over whether to tell Izzy about the library visit or wait for Aubrey to come down first and just when she decided she'd tell Izzy, she was forestalled by a shout from Aubrey.

"Could you come up here, Penny?" he said.

Penny looked at Izzy. "Do you think he can't find the sink?"

"He asked for you specifically," said Izzy with a conspiratorial waggle of her eyebrows.

Penny sighed at her cousin's schoolyard behaviour and went up.

"What is it?"

"Are you living here now?" said Aubrey. He was on the landing, between the kitchenette and the toilet. "I just wondered if it needed a little tidying up."

"Hey, I only just moved in the other day."

He tapped his chest with his now clean fingers. "I mean,

as a decorator, I wondered if you needed a bit of decorating done."

"I don't think Mr Dinktrout will spring for that as well."

"But I could definitely do it for mate's rates. I'm thinking a simple off-white emulsion throughout could make this place look a lot more habitable, and I could sand down and treat the floorboards, no problem."

"I don't know if I'm staying here that long," said Penny honestly, thinking about Nanna Lem in hospital. The impression her grandma gave was definitely one of a temporary situation.

"I'm sorry to hear that."

"Really?" she said and wished she hadn't. It sounded vain and a poor attempt to fish for compliments.

"This town needs young blood. And young local blood."

"My parents are in Nottingham and I've been working in London."

"But you're a local originally," he pointed out. He wandered through to the workshop space. "Now, this is a lovely room." He ran his hands over the plastered walls. "Lovely space, and original too." He stopped, spotting some of the vintage sewing magazines scattered among the clutter. "A paint job throughout. A contrast colour on the woodwork including that picture rail. I could frame some of the covers or patterns from these magazines. That would look nice."

"Actually, it would," said Penny, also thinking it would spur her and Izzy to tidy the place. "You think you can provide us with a quote."

He nodded amiably, took out his phone and snapped a few pictures.

"Show him your bedroom!" Izzy shouted from downstairs.

Penny sighed. "Yes. Come see my current digs, Aubrey. And if by some horrible mistake, I end up staying here longer, you can quote me for redecorating that too."

As the afternoon wore on and trade in the town slowed (with little effect on the practically non-existent trade in Cozy Crafts) Penny made preparation notes on her laptop for the workshop Izzy was going to run.

"Hey, Izzy. Does the shop's insurance cover events like this, do you know?"

There was such a long pause that Penny looked up to make certain Izzy had heard the question.

"Insurance?" Izzy said.

Penny experienced a small chill of dawning realisation. "There *is* some insurance covering the shop, yes? Public liability at the very least?"

Izzy chewed a lip. "It's possible, yeah."

Penny nodded. 'Possible' meant that maybe Nanna Lem had organised it in the past. Penny flicked frantically through paperwork, searching for clues. A couple of hours later she had established that the policy had expired, but she had been able to renew it over the phone and make sure that it did indeed cover events like their planned workshop. She wondered how many other surprises like this lay in store.

"Next thing we need to do is carry out a risk assessment."

"What? Just for a little workshop?" Izzy complained.

"Yes. This will get easier for future events, but for now we just need to list all the things that might go wrong and think of ways to mitigate them."

"Oh right. I'll start," said Izzy. "Rogue bulldozer! Laser-eyed cats! Zombie apocalypse!"

Penny's hands were poised over the keyboard. "Shall we start with slips, trips and falls? As our guests carry out the day's activities, are there any hazards that might cause them to have a fall?"

"No."

"Yes! There are stairs they need to climb and there are power cables for the sewing machines. We need to write something in this document to show that we've thought about how to make those things safe."

Izzy huffed. "Is there a line in there that talks about the danger of the fun police sucking all the joy out of a thing?"

"Izzy, this is non-negotiable! You might think it's boring, but we cannot ignore the safety needs of our visitors."

Penny continued through the document, making adjustments to the workshop space as she went. She tried to ignore the simmering resentment that radiated off Izzy.

21

I zzy walked into the Saturday editorial meeting at Miller Fields sheltered accommodation. "Hobnob alert!" She held up a fresh pack of biscuits and was pleased to hear several appreciative noises.

"On a plate please, Izzy," said Glenmore.

Izzy rolled her eyes and fetched a plate. This was a ruse, they all knew it. Each of the staff had a method for securing the maximum number of biscuits. Izzy's method was the straightforward one of cramming them into her mouth as quickly as she could. Tariq would open the packet clumsily so that several biscuits 'fell' into his hand. Annalise would declare that it wasn't worth fastening the packet up, so she might as well eat 'the last few'. Glenmore would insist upon a plate, spread a number of biscuits onto it, as if he intended to share them, and then he would put the plate somewhere that only he could reach.

Once biscuits and drinks were served, Glenmore held up

his notes. "There's an item on the agenda called World Book Day. Why on earth do we need a special day for books?"

"It's always been there," said Tariq.

"Not when I was a boy, it wasn't!"

"True, but it's not exactly a brand new thing Glenmore," said Izzy. "It's to encourage reading. Children in schools get free books, and they're encouraged to dress up as characters."

"The library will get involved too, it's a really fun event," said Annalise. "There will be special displays, we'll be doing some readings for the younger children and staff will dress up too. I was Timmy the dog from the Famous Five books last year. My costume went a bit funny in the wash, so I will be Hairy Maclary this year."

"Free books! Well, that'll be why the potholes aren't getting filled." Glenmore looked unimpressed.

Izzy didn't bother to explain that the council didn't organise World Book Day and that, consequently, it was not funded by pothole money. "What it will mean for us is the chance to get lots of great pictures of children in their costumes. People always enjoy the chance to see their kids in the paper."

"Should we be encouraging such indulgence?" asked Glenmore. "Soft parents producing soft offspring, hardly fitting for the country of Kitchener and Gordon and Clive of India."

Izzy bit down on the urge to scream that yes of course they should indulge such things, and that furthermore, it was rather odd for a British Jamaican to uphold dubious colonial warriors as paragons of British virtue. She said none of that and instead said, "It's only once a year."

"Very well." Glenmore pursed his lips. "Tariq, I would like you to get along to the school and take photos."

"On it!" Tariq was buzzing, as he was rarely tasked with anything more challenging than taking minutes for Glenmore.

Glenmore consulted his notes. "Now, do we have Madame Zelda's horoscopes for the upcoming edition?"

"Madame Zelda is on the case," said Izzy. "She has assured me that the horoscopes will be ready, even though she is busy with many other engagements."

The group all nodded.

"What other engagements does Madame Zelda have?" asked Tariq.

"Tariq, have you not heard of GDPR and privacy? To divulge details of Madame Zelda's professional engagements would be highly unprofessional of me," said Izzy.

Tariq stared, but Izzy did not break eye contact until he looked away.

"Very good," said Glenmore. "I need to buy a new umbrella, so I look forward to seeing what colour will work best for Libra."

Izzy scribbled a note. "I'm sure she will cover that."

"Now, what about word nerd corner?"

Izzy leaned forward. "I'm thinking of tying word nerd corner in with World Book Day." She ignored Glenmore's raised eyebrows. "For example, the word 'genre' which has fairly simple roots in the Latin word 'genus' meaning 'sort' or 'type'. Annalise, 'genre' is a word that you probably use in the library every day to talk about books, but did you know that the ancient Greeks started it all? Aristotle wanted to organise books into poetry, drama or prose."

Annalise smiled and nodded. "That sounds good. I might run your column through the laminator and pop it on the library wall, Izzy! Our visitors like to see these fun facts."

Glenmore leaned forward. "Genre, genre. It's a bit French, isn't it? Maybe we should have a proper English word?"

"Glenmore, my love," said Annalise, "we'll fall back to the rule we've applied before. If it's in the Oxford English Dictionary then it's a word that we can use. You were happy with that rule last time."

"I still say English words are English words. No need to sully it with foreign imports."

"The English language is almost nothing but foreign imports, Glenmore."

"Poppycock!"

"Well, that's Dutch."

"Baloney!"

"Definitely Italian."

"Waffle and flannel, I say!"

"French and Welsh, I think," said Annalise after some thought.

Annalise winked at Izzy as Glenmore made some further grumbling sounds, but they were able to move on. And Glenmore consoled himself with an extra hobnob.

"We have proper news to put in the newspaper, you know," he said. "Roy Cotwin's unfortunate death is still the talking point of the town."

"A character portrait of the deceased?" suggested Tariq.

"It would be nothing but a character assassination in his case," said Annalise.

"Papers publish facts," Glenmore insisted.

"And horoscopes," said Annalise.

"Horoscopes are factual," insisted Izzy.

"It's a fact one wrote them," said Annalise. "That's the limit of it."

22

Penny was initially surprised to discover that Izzy was an occasional churchgoer, although she wasn't entirely sure why she shouldn't have expected this. The church was a vital part of the community in rural Suffolk, and the pair of them had been sent off to Sunday School every week as kids. But Penny had always felt the family's faith was a lip service thing, limited to births, deaths, marriages and the occasional Christmas nativity play. Not with Izzy, apparently.

The discovery had come about because Penny had assumed Izzy would want a day off from sewing on Sunday and had suggested it on Saturday.

"Oh, no. I think we will need to crack on with Lorina's dress. If she's a vengeful murderess then we'd best not be on her bad side."

Penny had told Izzy all that she had heard and discovered, but wasn't sure if Izzy believed her.

"I can't come until after church though," Izzy said.

"Church?"

"The big pointy building with all the Christians in it. It's just behind the marketplace."

"I know what a church is," said Penny but, again, she wasn't sure if Izzy believed her.

And so it was that Izzy arrived back at the shop shortly after one o'clock bearing two bowls of treacle sponge with custard.

"Mum says you need feeding up," said Izzy.

Penny hadn't had a chance to drop in on her Auntie Pat and Uncle Teddy yet. Or, to be more precise, she had been avoiding family. If you looked hard, there were a lot of them. And the more you looked, the more of them there were. And Penny felt pulled in two directions, by the need to get the shop shipshape for Nanna Lem and the need to see this whole arrangement as temporary. She was here to do a good favour and then get out of here, back to London.

"Thank your mum for me," said Penny and ate a corner of deliciously gooey warm treacle sponge to show willing.

Penny's confidence with dressmaking was growing. Using the sewing machine didn't feel like such an alien experience any more, but she was filled with dread when the time came to cut into the lovely blue fabric.

"What if I spoil it?" she said to Izzy.

"I'm watching. It will be fine. We know that the pattern fits Lorina, so all we need to do now is make it up accurately in this lovely fabric."

Penny used the large tailor's shears to make the first cut.

They were very sharp and it was extremely satisfying to feel them snicking through the crisp cotton. "I think I understand why people get so protective of their dressmaking scissors. It's lovely when they work so well."

"Uh-huh. And rage-inducing when they don't. We get the scissors professionally sharpened every few months."

"Do we offer that service to our customers?"

Izzy frowned in thought. "No, but I guess we could. You know, I'm not even sure how many dressmakers there are round here. I mean, how many people even own scissors like this?"

Penny stood up and put the scissors flat on the fabric. She pulled out her phone and snapped a picture. "Let's get people to show us, shall we? I'll make a social media post asking people to share their favourite fabric scissors."

"A beauty contest for scissors, I love it!"

Through the afternoon, Penny was increasingly thrilled to see the blue Alice dress coming together into something recognisable. Izzy had coaxed her through the tricky part of setting the sleeve and having conquered that, it seemed as though everything else should be a breeze.

She was about to ask what they should do next when Izzy pointed out it was dark outside. Six hours of sewing had flown by and now evening was upon them.

"We'll leave the rest until tomorrow," said Izzy. "Look at it with fresh eyes."

Izzy left, taking the empty treacle sponge bowls with her. There was a strange feeling in Penny's chest, and it took her a moment to realise it was a burning need to keep on sewing.

She was excited to get the dress finished, to see the complete design done and put on its waiting customer. She had undoubtedly caught the dressmaking bug.

"Well, who'd a thunk?" she asked her reflection in the shop window, and locked up for the night.

23

As Izzy took her circuitous cycle route to work the following morning, she couldn't help noticing yet more excitement in Double Street. It wasn't another death, or at least, she assumed it wasn't, but it was centred on Roy Cotwin's house. A man on the ground was having a rather loud and frank conversation with a man up a ladder. The man on the ground was wearing a sharp-looking suit and waving papers in his hand, and looked very much like a solicitor or somesuch. The man up the ladder, who had just started painting the top of the house wall, was Aubrey the painter.

"I'm just doing what I'm told," Aubrey called down to the man.

"And I'm telling you that you aren't allowed to do that!" the suited man shouted up at him.

"Then you'll have to take that up with Mr Dinktrout."

"Put *you're* the one doing the painting!"

Aubrey didn't disagree, instead applying an extra splodge of paint to the wall as further evidence. The solicitor-type man did a funny little dance of annoyance and stomped off.

Aubrey smiled, not unkindly, shook his head, and then saw Izzy in the road astride her bike.

"Solicitor," Aubrey explained.

"Ah, thought so."

"I've got something for you," he said as he made his way down.

"What was that about anyway?" asked Izzy, though she thought she could guess.

Aubrey jerked his thumb at the house. "Mr Dinktrout wanted me to repaint this eyesore. But Roy Cotwin's probate solicitor objects to us doing anything until the estate is sorted out or something."

"Sounds like a thorny problem."

Aubrey shrugged happily. "I just paint things."

Izzy looked up. Aubrey had only made slight in-roads on the paint job, but she could already see the difference between the two pinks. The existing paint was the pink of a princess dress or a gaudy plastic unicorn. The new pink was much more subtle, almost floral.

"Suffolk pink?" she asked.

"Of course."

"Do they still make it with cow's blood?"

"That's a myth," said Aubrey. "Put cow's blood in limewash and it separates out into a horrid mess. I go with the theory that the original colour came from adding burnt clay ochre or brick dust."

Suffolk pink could be found on houses throughout the county. It added extra colour to the green and brown landscape and it was one of the things that tourists associated with the area.

"Mr Dinktrout eager to correct Roy's 'mistake' then?" said Izzy.

"You can say that again," replied Aubrey, and then he caught the look in her eye. "Not a thing to wish a man dead over, though." He dipped into his big overall pocket and pulled out a couple of sheets of paper folded into quarters, which he handed to Izzy. "Quotes for the work on the shop and flat."

Izzy looked them over. The numbers were just numbers to her. Once you got over a certain amount of money all numbers were equally huge. She'd let Penny take a look at that.

"The workshop. You think you could have it decorated by this Saturday?"

Aubrey laughed. "I'm sorry. I'm chocka. Looking at three weeks ahead, if not more."

Izzy put the quote in her bicycle's basket. She'd have to bring some order to the workshop herself, then.

"She's single, you know," she said.

"What?" replied Aubrey. "I didn't ask."

"Ask what?" said Izzy and cycled off.

During the morning, between dealing with the very few customers that came in and taking a delivery of catalogues from the postman, Penny continued to work on the Alice in Wonderland dress. She was tackling it with increasing skill and certainty — or at least, she was until Izzy told her they'd now need to use the overlocker to stop the seams from fraying.

"What do you mean I need to use the overlocker?" said Penny with sudden nervousness.

Izzy smiled patiently.

"I've seen that thing," said Penny. "It's more like a waste disposal than a sewing machine, it's terrifying! There's no way that a Victorian dressmaker would have used one of those."

"True," said Izzy. "We could do all the seams by hand, but it would take a lot longer and we'd have to charge Lorina a lot more money. Take my word, the overlocker is what we need here. You'll soon get used to it."

Penny did not appear convinced. The speed with which overlocker worked was alarming, and even worse, it cut away some of the fabric as it went, so mistakes could be irreversible.

"We'll sit together and take it slowly," Izzy reassured her. "Practise on some scraps until you're confident and then we can do the dress. In fact, the overlocker is different to a normal sewing machine because you can use it with no fabric at all, just to get the feel of it. Try it now."

Penny sat in front of it and pressed the pedal with her foot. It snarled and chattered, multiple needles and levers whizzing about in their complicated dance. It made a chain of thread which grew out of the back. Penny could see the tiny knife that would cut the fabric.

"Ready for some fabric?" asked Izzy.

"Yes." Penny took the scrap that Izzy handed her. It was quite a large scrap.

"Let's neaten the edge of this. Feed it under and watch how it works."

Penny did as instructed and saw how the chain of thread was now a neat finish on the fabric. The knife chopped off the excess fabric to the right, so the stitching was perfectly aligned with the edge.

"See if you can make it remove just one or two millimetres from the edge," said Izzy.

Penny had been careful to keep her fingers well away from the working parts of the machine, and it was clear she was nervous about whether she could control the fabric properly, but Izzy knew it was relatively easy once she gained confidence.

"I feel like I need to watch where it's stitching," said Penny. "But at the same time, I've got to watch where it's chopping and watch where it's feeding in. That's three things at once, and I only have two eyes, and they tend to look in the same direction. But I think I'm getting the hang of it."

"You certainly are. We'll practise corners and curves and then you'll be ready for the dress. I thought I might start on the mood board."

"Mood board?"

"For the Fabricabulous website."

"Um, I thought you were going to get the workshop ready for the kid's event."

"I can do both."

Penny made a doubtful noise. Penny struck Izzy as a woman composed mostly of doubtful noises and hesitations. She needed a bit of self belief. Izzy didn't do doubtful noises. When, as a child, she'd set out to trap the mythical singing mice, or make her own hot air balloon, or build her own igloo, she'd never harboured any doubt. True, she had also failed in all of those endeavours, but whatever the cause of those failures, it could not have been doubt.

Izzy couldn't wait to tackle the mood board. And she knew that she could prepare for the children's group and do the fun mood board task at the same because she was a master of multi-tasking and would figure out a way to make them both happen.

Leaving Penny with the overlocker, she went up and looked long and hard at the first floor workshop. Six tables, each with a sewing machine on it, was the vision she needed to aim for. She tried to estimate how much old stock and rubbish she would need to move out. It looked like a lot. She examined the fabrics that were in here. There was some sturdy cotton canvas in bright colours that would be perfect for making tote bags, so that would stay. There was an enormous roll of calico as well. Lovely cheap calico. Calico that came in a generous sixty inch width... Izzy smiled as she realised that she could solve several problems with one creative solution. She was going to make a mood board that the children could help her with, and what's more, she would use it to hide a load of messy storage in the same room.

She started by putting some large hooks into the skirting board at each corner of the back wall. Then she put some up on the picture rail sixty inches up.

"Izzy will now invent the calico false wall!" she announced to nobody at all, but she was brimming with pride at the idea. There was an eyelet kit downstairs, and a few minutes later she had set large eyelets into the ends of the calico, top and bottom. She hooked it into place on the left hand side of the back wall. It fit perfectly.

Now all she had to do was pile up all the rest of the room's junk flush to the wall and she could wrap it in calico, so it would look like a cool minimalist interior (with a few lumpy bits). She made sure the fabric rolls wrapped in plastic were on the outside, because of what she planned to inflict on that lovely minimalist wall when the kids were here. After half an hour she had dragged everything into place, all temporarily wedged behind chairs and tables so that it wouldn't topple forward. Eventually she was ready to bring the calico round, wrapping everything behind its creamy bland facade, and then she would hook it onto the right hand side of the wall. When she had applied the eyelets, she pulled the fabric over all of the stuff that she was hiding and fastened it in place in the corner.

"Result!" she crowed. Now she was able to line the tables up neatly, a sewing machine on each. Penny would be so impressed.

24

Rain came in that afternoon and drove all the shoppers from the streets. The raindrops thrummed on the shop window, a dull pitter-patter, a soundtrack to Penny's work.

Penny finished trimming the loose threads and took the dress over to the ironing board. Izzy had shown her how to press seams, which was nothing at all like normal ironing.

"We take the tailor's ham," she said in her best rasping psycho killer voice as she laid the dress over the sawdust-filled tailor's ham, "and then we press the pointy end of the iron into the seam as if we are gouging the eyes of our enemies!"

"I'm worried by how much you're taking that to heart," said Izzy.

"It's sort of satisfying, but I think you knew that when you told me what to do," laughed Penny. "It makes such a difference, too. It looks so crisp and well-finished."

Penny continued pressing and finally held up the finished dress. "It looks even better than the picture I'd had in my head. Let's put it on the mannequin with the apron!"

They dressed the mannequin and stood back to admire it. It was, perhaps, a little less than perfect but, by gosh, it was a made to measure pale blue Alice in Wonderland dress, complete with a deep padded hem, gathered sleeves and hand-made bias binding on the neckline.

"I've got to say, that looks stunning," said Izzy. "Well done Penny! You made your first commission."

"Honestly Izzy, this is one of the best things I have ever done, and you helped me all the way through."

"Think about what you want to make next. Something for yourself that you can wear in the shop, maybe. I'll give Lorina a call and tell her that her outfit is ready."

Penny picked up her phone to take some pictures of the dress. "Oh look, have you seen how many people have shared pictures of their favourite scissors?" She showed Izzy. "All different shapes and sizes. People are even asking about sharpening. I think we might have hit a nerve."

"I'll get in touch with the sharpening guy, see if we can set something up!" said Izzy. "I should do a feature for the Frambeat Gazette. Oh, there's a copy of the latest edition on the counter. You should check out your horoscope."

25

Izzy liked to leave customers to browse. She knew that some people were irritated by too much attention. She kept her eyes on the laptop as she worked on the Frambeat article she was writing, but her ears were tuned to the whispered conversation between two children looking through the fancy dress costumes. The teenage girl was in charge of the small boy.

"These are all too expensive. You can have five pounds. That's what Mum said."

"Yeah but —"

"—No buts! She said."

The girl came over to the counter. "Have you got any cheaper costumes than these?" she asked Izzy. "He needs something for World Book Day."

Izzy gave a thoughtful nod. "I can try to help. What's your budget?"

"Five pounds and not a penny more. Mum said Mrs Ockenden got a wedding dress costume for next to nothing."

"Not quite," said Izzy. "But it will surprise you what can be done with five pounds." She stepped away from the counter. "What type of costume would you like? Do you have a favourite book character?"

"BFG," mumbled the boy. He seemed unsure about this choice, eyeing the girl.

"The big friendly giant!" said Izzy. "Great choice. Let me think about that. Actually, I might just get a picture so I can be clear what we're after."

The boy sidled round as Izzy found a picture on her phone. He pointed when she found a good one. "That one!"

"So, he has green trousers, a scruffy brown waistcoat and big ears. Have you got any of those things already at home?"

The boy shook his head, but his sister made a thoughtful noise. "I've got some green cropped trousers. You could wear them with a belt, I suppose."

"Great! that leaves us with the waistcoat and the ears." Izzy stared around the shop for inspiration. The paper bags on the counter snagged her attention for a moment. A waistcoat could easily be cut from a bag. She'd seen those famous vintage pictures of Debbie Harry wearing a black bin liner cut into a waistcoat. Paper was too easily damaged, though; it would never make it through World Book Day. "Hah!" Izzy realised that she had a different kind of bag in just the right colour. She raced upstairs and fetched one of the damaged pillowcases. It was made from brown cotton and was exactly what she needed.

Izzy took the pillowcase to the cutting table and chopped

off the open end to about the length she judged the waistcoat should be. Then she cut armholes into the sides, and cut up the middle of the front, opening it out at the top to make the right shape for the neck.

"Try this on."

The boy shrugged on the waistcoat. It hung on him in exactly the right way. He gave her a wide grin.

"Now, we need ears. I have an idea for those." Izzy had noticed some of the old-fashioned haberdashery Penny had dropped into the junk box, and had been wondering what they might do with it. The thing that she had in mind was in one of those boxes, but which one was it? "I'll just need a moment to find what I'm after. Can we have your headband?"

Izzy addressed the question to the teenage sister. Her hand went to her head as she stared in confusion. "But I'm wearing it!"

"We need it for the ears."

The girl scowled but removed her headband, a plastic thing that arched over her head.

Izzy had ferreted through nearly all the boxes, grunting with frustration, before her hand closed around the squishy packet she'd been searching for. "Here we go."

She put the packet on the table and opened it.

"Beauty forms?" said the girl.

"These are old-fashioned bra pads," said Izzy, "but they are flesh-coloured and I think they will make great ears."

She threaded a hand needle with doubled-over thread and leaned on the table, squishing the springy foam disc into place at the base of the headband. "I'll get it on here as securely as I can. It will take me a few minutes." She squished and stitched, going over and over so that it wouldn't move. She held it up and the two children nodded with approval. "Good! I'll do the other side."

Once Izzy had finished, she stepped back to admire her work on the head of the boy. "I think we nailed it."

The sister was so impressed that she forgot to scowl at the loss of her headband. Once the boy had checked himself in the mirror, he couldn't stop smiling.

"That'll be five pounds then," said Izzy. "Told you we could do it. Always up for a challenge. Tell your friends!"

26

P enny flicked through the slender copy of *Framlingham's History in Pictures* Lorina had loaned her, while sipping her breakfast coffee. She had been in the town for precisely a week, and was starting to settle into a happy routine. There was no news of Nanna Lem coming out of hospital yet, and Penny mulled over the idea of taking a trip back to Ipswich to see her grandma and get an update.

The picture history book had photos of people and buildings from across the last hundred and forty years. Photos of early twentieth century market traders in their white aprons and flat caps drew a smile from her. The outfits might be different these days but the character of the town was very much the same. Unlike other towns, Framlingham had hardly changed at all in the past century. A picture of a grocer's shopping list and bill of sale for plants showed that prices had risen dramatically over the decades, and sure, its edges had expanded outwards with new housing developments on all sides, but the town itself remained a constant.

She gave up on the history book and turned her attention to the free newspaper Izzy had brought in at the beginning of the week. Local newspapers generally struck Penny as extremely dull, full of contentless stories about roadworks or girl guide activities or third-prize marrows. Nonetheless, it would be a good way to become familiar with local events and personalities. She skimmed the adverts for landscape gardeners and conservatory sales, but read all of the articles. It was an entertaining mixture of reviews, advice and even some local history. It would be useful to understand what sort of readership the newspaper had, and whether it might be a useful platform for Cozy Crafts to advertise or feature.

She paused at the horoscope page. Penny wasn't superstitious, but she always felt compelled to check what the stars thought should be happening to Aries. Sometimes it was a useful opportunity to reflect on what was actually happening.

Don't be so hung up on following rules. You will have a lot more fun in life if you accept a few risks.

She frowned. How very odd! Perhaps she had overreacted a little when Izzy had poo-pooed the risk assessment. She should probably apologise.

"I know how they did it," declared Izzy, coming into the shop front bearing several glasses and a jug of water on a tray.

"Who did what?"

"The murderer."

"Roy's death?"

"Have there been any other murders since?"

"I didn't realise we were still dwelling on that."

Izzy put the tray on the counter. "You said that Stuart opened the champagne and then it was poured into glasses and then they came round and each person took one."

"That's right."

Izzy poured out three glasses of water, humming a little tune as she did. "All the same. None of them any different, right?"

She indicated the other items on the tray: a pack of straws and a caddy of sugar.

"Pop a green straw in that one. And a yellow straw in that one. And..." She took the blue straw and stuck it in the sugar. "Now this sugar is the poison."

"Right."

"It's not actually poison. It's just poison for the purposes of my demonstration."

"Good to know."

She lifted the straw out with her fingertip over the top and placed it into the third glass. When she let go, a little cloud of crystal appeared at the bottom of the glass.

"Most of the poison is still in the straw so when Roy drinks through it..."

"So, not poisoned champagne but a poisoned straw?"

"Exactly. Ingenious, isn't it?"

Penny was about to offer an opinion on the ingenious nature of things, and point out that it was rather odd to put straws in champagne in the first place, when the shop door jingled and Lorina walked in. Her eyes latched onto the Alice in Wonderland dress at once and she approached it in a stunned stoop, arms out wide.

"Oh! Oh! It's marvellous. Simply wonderful! Oh, frabjous day, as one ought to say."

"You like it?" said Penny with a light nervousness.

"Oh, callooh callay, dear girl. It's simply gorgeous."

"Come try it on," said Izzy and ushered her upstairs, carrying the dress for her.

Penny looked at the drinks on the tray, and the drinking straws. It was, she had to admit, an ingenious method of delivering poison, but she could not recall Roy drinking his champagne through the straw or indeed anyone specifically giving him a particular straw. The problem of how one drink might be poisoned and the others not and how that one drink had been put into his hand remained as before.

Soon enough, Izzy and Lorina returned, the older woman swishing her skirts like a little girl.

"This is the best," she said. "The very best of all things. It will be my outfit for this World Book Day and every World Book Day to come. And World Book Day might not be until tomorrow but I'm going to wear it now. It's that lovely."

"Thank you," said Penny, who had to admit, it sat on the woman's slender frame well. If Lewis Carroll had ever written a book entitled *Alice, the Later Years*, then he couldn't have asked for a better Alice than this.

Lorina opened her purse and started counting bank notes onto the counter. She saw the open book.

"Seen it yet?" she said.

"Seen what?" asked Penny.

"Damning evidence," said Lorina conspiratorially. "I'm

actually off up to see Stuart in a bit. I might eventually put him out of his misery."

"Misery?"

Lorina smiled brightly, but there was a cruel edge to that smile. "Mind if I...?" She picked up one of the glasses and sucked at the straw. "Ooh, sweet. Wasn't expecting that. But Alice did get into trouble for eating and drinking things without thinking first."

She counted out the final bill and pushed it across to Penny. It was, in a single transaction, far more cash than all the money the shop had taken since her arrival.

"And I meant to tell you," said Lorina. "A funny thing happened. The police came round to the library yesterday. They asked if they could have a look in our cupboards."

"Pardon?" asked Izzy.

"Looking for rat poison, they were," said Lorina. "Seemed to think we had boxes of it stashed away somewhere. Of course, they found nothing."

"Nothing?" said Penny.

"Nothing," replied Lorina emphatically. Her gaze lingered on Penny for a long, long moment and then she giggled like the little girl she was dressed as and twirled out of the shop, her own clothes in a paper shopping bag under her arm.

Neither of them said anything for a long while.

"She murdered him, didn't she?" said Penny.

"Maybe."

"She murdered Roy Cotwin because he was making her life hell."

"Or had found out she was embezzling the library."

"And there's something going on between her and Stuart Dinktrout."

"Gonna 'put him out of his misery' she said," Izzy added thoughtfully.

"That sounds ominous."

They stared out of the window some more, even though Lorina had long gone.

"But, dang, she looked good in that dress," said Izzy, and Penny couldn't help but nod in agreement.

27

B y noon, Izzy had finished the waistcoat for Arabella the pig. Having packed it carefully into her bicycle basket, she cycled up to Dinktrout Nurseries for the fitting.

Stuart Dinktrout was waiting for her when she turned up on her colourful bicycle. She saw him eyeing it, but he said nothing as she locked it into a rack.

"You have it?" he asked.

"I have it," said Izzy, taking the waistcoat, a tub of apple slices and a bag out of her basket.

"I will join you for the fitting, if you don't mind," he said.

Izzy smiled. "It could be a bit boring. Are you sure?"

She had secretly been hoping to pass a pleasant hour or so reading some decent poetry to Arabella and getting some pictures of the pig wearing her new waistcoat. She had printed a selection of things to read out, curious to understand Arabella's preferences. Would it be the gentle, well-loved cadence of WWII-era John Betjeman? Would it be the biting social media satire of Brian Bilston? Or would it be some nonsense lyrics from the Alice in Wonderland book they'd been using as a reference for the dress?

Izzy scowled when she realised that Stuart was holding that wretched pamphlet of his own dreadful poetry. She should have brought earplugs.

"And here she is!" Stuart cooed as they walked through the door into the indoor pig palace. Arabella trotted over to greet them. "What a champion my girl is!"

Izzy put her bag on the floor and pulled out the waistcoat. "We'll waste no time, Arabella. Here it is!" She held it up. It featured a brocade fabric in a mixture of deep plummy purples. "Do you like the colour? I think it's going to look amazing."

"Perhaps I need to read some poetry to get Arabella to stand still for you?" said Stuart.

Arabella stood still as a statue. Not a quiver of movement could be seen in her body. Izzy took it as the most obvious protest that the little pig was able to muster in the face of Stuart's awful verse. She tried not to laugh as she held the waistcoat in place and fastened the buttons.

"I brought a mirror, so that you can see yourself," said Izzy. She reached into her bag and pulled out a large hand mirror, angling it so that Arabella could see her reflection.

Arabella gave a squeal of delight, and moved gently from side to side so that she could admire herself.

"May I take a picture?" Izzy asked.

"You may," said Stuart, although Izzy hadn't been asking him.

Arabella positioned herself so that Izzy could see the waistcoat to full effect.

"Have you done modelling before, Arabella? You're such a natural! I might have a slice of apple for you."

Izzy pulled a tub from her bag and emptied the slices into her palm. Arabella snuffled them daintily into her mouth and gave a grateful snort as they disappeared.

"Very good," said Stuart. "I shall be needing some more of these by the way, in different colours and patterns."

"You do like to spoil her, don't you?"

"I have no one else."

Izzy looked at him. "Never met someone you wanted to share your life with?"

"A very personal question."

"Sorry."

"I was engaged once," he said, distantly.

"Oh."

"She broke it off, though, days before the wedding. By letter of all things. People can be so cruel."

"Oh, I see," said Izzy, regretting having asked.

Stuart held his hands out wide. "All this could have been hers."

Izzy wasn't sure whether he meant the Dinktrout empire or just Arabella's piggy palace. Was his piggy really a substitute for the wife he never had?

His gaze returned from whichever far off place it had been too. "But, yes, more waistcoats. Arabella has a number of appearances and shows coming up."

"What kind of shows?" asked Izzy. "Does she win prizes?"

Stuart gave a huff. "She should! There was some

ridiculous objection lodged at the all-county fair last month. That damnable idiot Mountjoy tried to cast doubt upon my darling's classification as a micro pig. Tried to convince the judges that she's just an undersized mini."

"No!"

"It's true. Mountjoy has a number of micro pigs, but I know for a fact that he just overfeeds his mini-micros."

Izzy wasn't keeping up with this conversation. She had no idea which size was which, and she really didn't care, but she did want to get those extra orders, as waistcoats were simple to make, all the more so now they had a workable pattern for Arabella. "We can personalise a waistcoat too, did you know that?" she said.

Stuart raised an eyebrow, clearly not all that impressed, but Arabella gave a loud squeak and ran in an excited circle.

"Well, that sounds like something we need. My best girl has to look her best, eh?"

A young garden centre worker entered the pen and beckoned Stuart. There was brief, hushed conversation.

"Speaking of cruel people, I have a small matter to attend to," he said to Izzy. "I'll return with the cash for the additional waistcoats."

Stuart left and Izzy was alone with Arabella. "Well, you do look very lovely in your waistcoat," she told the handsome pig. "We have a few minutes alone now. I want to get your opinion on a few poems. How about we start with some Lewis Carroll nonsense?"

She opened the Alice in Wonderland book and read Carroll's verse.

. . .

How doth the little crocodile
  Improve his shining tail,
  And pour the waters of the Nile
  On every golden scale!
  How cheerfully he seems to grin,
  How neatly spreads his claws,
  And welcomes little fishes in,
  With gently smiling jaws!

Izzy was put in mind momentarily of the smile Lorina had given when she said she was going to put Stuart out of his misery. It was enough to make one shudder.

There was a strange sound from outside. Izzy couldn't be sure if was a human shout or the squawk of a bird but it faded as suddenly as it started. Izzy shrugged and was about to return to some poetic readings when, barely visible among the straw in the corner of Arabella's enclosure, she spotted a pair of amber eyes looking at her.

"Ah, you must be the infamous escape artiste Percy," said Izzy.

A pink nose twitched in a white face.

"Excuse me," Izzy said to Arabella and put the book aside. She opened the tub of apples, offered another slice to Arabella and approached the rabbit with the rest.

"Care for some apple, Percy? And then we can get you back into your home."

Percy looked at her, twitched his nose once more and ran out. Acting on sheer instinct, Izzy gave chase. She emerged into bright winter sunshine in time to see Percy the rabbit scampering through a stand of potted climbers. Izzy pushed her way through the bamboo cane supports, stepped over a short fence that was in her way and found herself in the garden ornament section of the garden centre. Here there were rabbits but only pottery ones, alongside hedgehogs and badgers. Further along there were the peculiar metal ornaments of much larger creatures. There was no sign of Percy.

However, there was someone here. A person sprawled out on the stone path between the selections of ornaments. A metal flamingo lay on the ground next to her on one side, and on the other, a selection of local history books had spilled out in a line as if flung out as she fell. Izzy rushed over to see if she could help but one look told her she was far too late.

Izzy had of course recognised the woman as soon as she'd seen her. She herself had helped her into that delightful blue dress only a couple of hours before.

28

Penny set a pair of steaming coffee mugs on the counter.

"Hey," she said.

Izzy looked up slowly, as if her mind had been somewhere else entirely.

"Hey," she replied quietly.

"You sleep okay last night?"

The question appeared to be too complex for Izzy to answer right now. She put her hands around the warm mug.

"Not sure if I've ever seen a dead body before," she said. "Apart from the one I found in my mum's garden."

"You found a dead body in your mum's garden?"

Izzy shook her head. "Turned out it was a scarecrow, blown over from Pott's field. I can't believe Lorina is dead."

"But she was dead?"

Izzy nodded. "I did the things. I felt for a pulse. I shouted for help. I was still there when the ambulance came.

Someone was saying what a tragedy it was that a flamingo should fall off the display and clonk her —" She stopped and took a deep breath. "Clonk. What a way to go."

Penny didn't like to see her cousin so discombobulated, though she too was shocked and saddened. She was distractingly worried that part of her sadness was that Lorina had never got to show off her new dress on World Book Day.

"Maybe you should take the day off," she suggested.

"What about the customers?"

"What customers?"

Izzy pointed to the door. There was a small queue of young people outside.

"It's not even nine," said Penny.

Izzy went and unlocked the door. A line of children came in.

"Where are your parents?" asked Penny.

"Mum's in the Co-op," said the boy at the head of the queue. "She gave me this and said that I'm to come and get one of your World Book Day outfits for a fiver."

"Five pounds," said Penny as the child placed the money onto the counter. "We don't do costumes for a fiver."

Izzy made a guilty noise.

Penny glanced at Izzy. "Do you know something about this?"

"Huh. Well, you know me, I do like a challenge." And there was fresh lightness in Izzy's tone, a distraction from the upsets of yesterday that Penny didn't question any further.

"It's World Book Day and I need something," said the boy.

Izzy walked round and looked the boy up and down. "What books do you like reading?"

"Gangsta Granny," said the boy.

Izzy consulted her phone for a reference picture. "This book looks excellent. You'd recommend it, then?"

The boy gave a solemn nod.

"I can see what we need to do. That top you're wearing now will work, I think. If we make you a skirt and a mask, then I think everyone will know who you are, yes?"

Penny coughed lightly. "And we can do this for five pounds, can we?"

"What did I say about liking a challenge? Come over here with me, young man, and we'll look through the remnants for your skirt."

"The rest of you..." Penny addressed the other children. "Are you all here for cheap World Book Day costumes."

There were noises of assent.

"Then wait there and we'll be with you shortly."

Penny watched as Izzy rummaged through the wooden bin that contained the leftover pieces from the end of a fabric roll, or pieces with faults, all priced cheaply. Izzy pulled out a piece of flowery fabric and held it up.

"Floral corduroy! Very Gangsta, if you ask me. Shall we see how it looks?" She wrapped it around the boy's waist and nodded. "I'm going to add an elastic waistband and a popper so that you can just wrap it round. Does that work?"

"Yes. Don't forget the mask."

"Penny!" shouted Izzy. "Go to the felt squares and find a black one. Make a template from paper that fits our customer's face and then cut it out from the felt. A small hole on each side and some elastic will finish the job. I'm off to make this garment. I'll be two minutes."

Penny did as Izzy suggested, and barely faltered as she drew the mask shape onto paper. She looked up and saw the boy's face. "What? Isn't this the right shape?"

"It's more like this," he said, taking the pencil and altering the shape of the eyes.

"Let's cut it out and try it for size."

Penny was mildly outraged that Izzy made it back with a basic but functional skirt before she and her helper had completed the simple mask, but the entire outfit was finished in a few minutes.

"Happy?" asked Izzy as the boy posed in front of the mirror.

"Yeah!" he said.

"One last thing," said Izzy, double-checking the picture on her phone. She pulled a paper bag from under the counter and wrote SWAG in large capitals. She jogged upstairs and came back down with the bag bulked out. She wrapped tape around it so that it wouldn't spill and handed it over. "No actual swag in there, it's just trimmings and threads from the overlocker."

The boy looked delighted at the extra prop and raced out of the shop to catch up with his mother.

"All for well under a fiver!" crowed Izzy.

They turned to the next child in the queue. It was not any regular queue, though: this one was part critique group, part ideas factory and part production line.

"I need someone who can cut circles out of a cardboard box!" shouted Izzy. "Penny, give them some boxes from the recycling and a plate to draw round. I need six if we're going to make a Very Hungry Caterpillar."

"Eight would be better," shouted a girl.

"You lot drive a hard bargain. Fine, eight it is."

Izzy romped back and forth, fabrics and haberdashery trailing in her wake. "I need a couple of you over here making beards. Sit down and copy me, yeah? We get the upholstery trim, as it's got a loopy beard look already and we need to fasten it onto some canvas tape so we can tie it round our ears, see?"

The beard team sat and made beards. Penny overheard some discussion as they worked, improving and embellishing the original design with flourishes of their own.

Penny tried to keep tabs on the items that were being used, although she was impressed that Izzy's promise to keep the costs under five pounds seemed to be holding water. Most of the outfits ended up using materials that cost around half that, so they still made some margin on the sale.

"Now, pirates, come over here. You don't all want to look the same, obviously, so decide which book you're from. Peter Pan, Treasure Island or whatever."

"I'm Captain Jack Sparrow!" declared a girl.

"Is that a book, though?" said Izzy. "Maybe it doesn't matter."

Penny couldn't help but think that the recently departed Lorina would have very much thought it did matter.

"The important thing is that each of you will have a different hat or bandana," Izzy told the children. "Let's look at some of the trimmings you might want to attach so you stand out from the crowd, shall we? Captain Jack Sparrow, we might want to make some dreadlocks to hang from yours." Izzy ripped open a packet for a cheap and nasty *Intergalactic Princess with spiral hairdo* and pulled out the hairpiece. "You can start unravelling the wigs and we'll stitch it onto a hat. A girl over there wants to be Anne Frank and her hair is blonde, so she'll need some of this too, but we should be able to get a set of pirate dreadlocks from it as well."

"Right," said Penny. She looked at the spiralled hair to see if she could re-fashion it. There was no doubt at all that the energy level in the shop was very high. Izzy was giving the pirates a quick lesson in threading a needle so that they could apply the shiny trim of their choice onto their headgear.

"Was there someone who wanted to be a Rotten Roman?" called Izzy. A boy walked over. She held up the dress left over from the knock-off Princess Leia outfit. "We'll add a purple drape to this and then you need to join the table over there for a head dress. I'll be over in a minute and we'll sort you out with your laurel crown."

Penny smiled at the industrious scene in the shop, but she was very slightly scandalised by the lack of parents. Were all of these children old enough to be roaming the shops on their own? Then she spotted a woman walking past and peering inside. She sent a thumbs-up to someone over the road. There were parents around, but they just weren't coming inside the shop. Was this because they knew very well that a fancy dress outfit for a fiver was a cheeky and unreasonable ask? Probably. She needed to channel Izzy's enthusiasm into something that would make a more sustainable income for the shop.

"It almost seems as if you could make up a pirate kit," she said, eyeing up the pirate table.

"Oh yeah, we could do that," said Izzy.

Penny grabbed a notepad and started jotting down some ideas based on the whirl of outfits being thrown together around her. If some of these designs were repeatable, they would be a useful demonstration to get Izzy on board with a more formal costing model. If they designed a pirate kit with an eyepatch and a customisable bandana, they could cost each element and add on a margin. Izzy's current method was chaotic and ad-hoc, although Penny had to admit it was effective. She was coming in well under the five pound budget every time.

And the act of throwing herself into a costume-making challenge had turned her thoughts away from Lorina's unfortunate demise. An accident, Izzy had said. For reasons she could not quickly articulate, Penny found that very hard to believe.

29

In the afternoon, Izzy set to work on her mood board for the yet-to-be-properly-developed shop website. It was something that definitely needed doing, and provided another welcome distraction from thoughts of Lorina's recent death. Izzy had found some old fabric sample books and a box of *Hello* magazines that she'd been given a while back. She was sitting cross-legged in the workshop room thinking hard about the personality of the website Fabricabulous.

She flicked through the magazines and paused at a picture of Julia Roberts. Julia Roberts, an elegant middle-aged woman, would be very welcome on the Fabricabulous website. A few pages later she found one of Katy Perry, sporting purple hair. Very fetching and individualistic. She cut out both pictures and pinned them to the calico. She was already bored of the magazines, so she went through a box that held scraps of fabric and trimmings. The strong jewel colours seemed right here, so she formed a large rectangular frame made of tiny colour-co-ordinated scraps.

She stepped back and decided that she liked the effect but it needed more content. What did Julia Roberts and Katie Perry have in common? A few moments of googling gave Izzy her answer.

"Yes! Both Scorpios!"

She drew the outline of a scorpion within the rectangle, ready for one of the kids to paint it.

She had stumbled across an approach to the mood board now, and she could definitely work with this. She would pick another star sign. What about Taurus? She had a quick look to see which celebrities came under the Taurus star sign. Duane 'The Rock' Johnson and Adele went up on the board. She pulled out some acid green and neon pink scraps to frame the Taurus area of the calico, then pencilled in a bull for a child to colour in.

This was working! She didn't need to represent every sign of the zodiac on the mood board, but four would be a good number, so she would include a water, earth, fire and an air sign. The website would have these four different areas, and each one would contain ideas, projects and of course supplies for each set of signs.

Already her mind was racing with the possibilities. Izzy thrilled with the genius of the idea and turned back to the colourful array of source materials. She decided that she would lay out the most skeletal of guidelines and then sort everything into piles of suitably coloured and themed content for each quadrant of the mood board. The creative freedom of children was a powerful thing. Adults lost that precious capability, constrained as they were by rules and worldly concerns. Izzy liked to think that she had held onto that childlike sense of wonder and creativity. With a little guidance, the workshop attendees would take this concept in interesting and unexpected directions, Izzy was certain of it.

30

I t was definitely the case that come Friday, the buzz of World Book Day had died down, and their one dressmaking commission had been completed and sold. However, they still had the children's workshop to prepare for the following day and the next exciting project was probably just around the corner. And yet... Izzy sighed.

Penny finished cutting and sorting strips of lacy trim.

"What's on your mind?" she said.

Izzy looked at her guiltily and then looked confused and then gave her a look that might have been constipation or might have been a strange reluctance and then finally said, "Do you think we'll ever see that dress again?"

"What dress? The Alice in Wonderland dress? Why?"

Izzy sighed once more. "It just doesn't seem fair. We made it together and it was lovely and Lorina only got to wear it for a few short hours before she died."

"And, just checking," said Penny, "obviously the tragedy

that the dress didn't get a proper outing is secondary to the tragedy that its owner is dead, right?"

"Obviously," said Izzy quickly. "But..."

"But...?"

"Do you think we could get it back if we asked nicely."

Penny made a sound that was part sympathy and part warning that Izzy's idea was not a good or tasteful one.

"I doubt we will," she said.

"I suppose not. And even if we did, what then? It was a fitted dress. And a woman died in it. People can be funny about things like that. And the fact that she put it on and died not long after... maybe that means its cursed."

"Dresses can't be cursed."

"Of course they can. Just like anything else."

"You have some funny notions, Izzy."

Izzy tutted. "What I find funny is that the entire team at the Frambeat Gazette seem to think her death was accidental."

"It could be."

"And we were so convinced that it was Lorina who killed Roy."

"So Lorina killed Roy and then Roy's ghost picked up a metal flamingo and whacked her on the head as revenge?"

"Or someone has good reason to kill them both," Izzy suggested.

"This is Fram," said Penny. "It's not murder central."

"I don't wish to speak ill of the dead, but they were both unlikeable characters in their own ways. Roy was a creep with an ugly house."

"Not exactly worthy of death."

"And Lorina wasn't shy about giving people her honest opinions."

"You mean her hatred of Disney and non-book related World Book Day costumes?"

"Tip of the iceberg."

Penny gave this some thought. "She made some strange-sounding threats to Stuart."

"Right. That 'putting him out of his misery' thing."

"Something to do with the history books he was looking at, I reckon."

"So, you agree," said Izzy. "Her death is suspicious. And we should probably look into it."

Penny was silent for a long moment and then sighed. "We're probably not going to get that dress back. Best we focus on tomorrow's workshop, eh?"

31

Penny was surprised when the first children turned up more than thirty minutes early for the workshop on Saturday morning. Their parents left them at the door, so there was no discussion. Her suspicions that this was little more than cheap childcare were not unfounded. The kids kept coming, and it became clear that there were more children than they had planned for.

"There are at least twenty of them!" hissed Penny to Izzy. "I've had to put name stickers on them, we'll never remember who's who."

Izzy gave a small shrug. "They can take turns, it'll be fine."

Penny herded them all upstairs into the workshop.

Izzy sorted them into groups.

"So, everyone will get to make a bag today, but we'll need to take turns with the machines. That doesn't mean you will be bored, though. There's cutting, pressing and sewing to do, and most exciting of all is helping paint our mood board. Who feels artistic?"

Penny had had no idea that Izzy was planning to include painting, but at least it enabled the kids to spread out.

"I made cardboard templates," she said. "You will each cut out pieces of the fabric that you like best out of these." Izzy patted a pile of fabric bolts. "Let me show you, so you can think about which one you'd like." Penny watched as Izzy held up colourful canvas designs. There was one featuring pink unicorns, another with sailing boats and a really delightful one that featured cartoon dogs and cats.

"I'll fetch more scissors," said Izzy and disappeared for a moment. She came back with several pairs of huge scissors.

"What are those?" asked Penny in horror.

"Tailors' shears. Classic design. Some of them are vintage."

"They are way too dangerous for kids, look!" Penny pointed at a young girl who was too small to get her hands into the handles, so she was operating them with two hands, swinging and chopping as if she were trimming the top of a hedge.

Izzy rolled her eyes. "We all learn by doing. That means using things that are dangerous sometimes. It's my workshop and I'll run it how I think best."

Penny intercepted and removed the giant scissors, but not before the girl had discovered that as well as being enormous, they were also incredibly sharp.

"She cut my strap!" It was Merida, the daughter of the librarian, and her dress hung loose on one side where the strap had been severed. Merida's face crumpled.

Penny grabbed the shears, and made sure she retrieved the other pairs, too. "Merida, we can help you with your dress, but first I need to make sure that these are well out of the way. Hey, Izzy. Emergency repair needed here."

Izzy beamed at Merida. "We can fix that. In fact, we will prove that fixes are very often better than the original. How would you like a flower on your strap?"

Merida's tears evaporated and she nodded with enthusiasm.

"I will use the machine in the room next door to make a flower, and I'll be back in a few minutes to fix the strap, yeah? Let me pop a safety pin on it for a moment so you can carry on working."

Izzy went to the smaller room. Penny saw an opportunity to mitigate the biggest risk of all to the wellbeing of everybody present. She hesitated for just a moment. and then she stepped out, pulled the door to that room closed and locked it.

"It's best you stay in there, Izzy," she shouted. "I need to make sure that these young people are working safely and right now you're acting like a bit of a liability."

"Because of the shears?"

"Yes, because of the shears."

Izzy hammered on the door as Penny went back inside the workshop, but she was confident that the combined noise of all the children drowned out the sound entirely.

"Who's finished cutting out the pieces from the cardboard template?"

It took a few minutes before everyone had the rectangular shapes cut out from their favoured fabrics, but

Penny was proud of herself when she saw that it was all done. She realised though that she had no clue what would come next. It was going to be a problem for her to run this workshop without Izzy's knowledge and confidence.

"Everybody sort your pieces neatly into size order and I will be back in one moment."

Penny scampered over to the locked door. "Izzy! Izzy! What do they need to do next?"

"Let me out and I can help!" said Izzy.

"Do you promise not to give them deadly weapons?"

"You can't keep them away from all potential harm."

"Fine, then stay there and tell me what to do."

"Sewing's a very practical skill. I need to show you!"

Penny couldn't run the risk, not until she'd got Izzy to commit to some basic rules of safety. "Why don't you look upon it as an intellectual challenge. If you can do this, then maybe one day you can write a book about sewing. Think very carefully about how you can describe it to me so that I can do it."

"Fine." Penny could hear the huff in Izzy's voice. "I'll play along until I've made this flower for Merida. Maybe then I can come out? Anyway, you need to take the handles, which are those two long thin pieces. Turn under a centimetre on each long side, then fold down the middle so all of the raw edges are inside. Use those little clips to hold it together neatly. Sew along the folded bits, then sew the other side and down the middle as well. It gets them all used to working the sewing machine."

Penny went back into the workshop room, where the children had started to whip each other with the long thin strips of fabric. Maybe the babysitting aspect of this job was going to be the toughest challenge after all. "Everyone!" she called. "Who can see where the little clips are?"

"Here!" A small blonde girl held up a little tin that was decorated with Beatrix Potter designs. It contained lots of colourful clips, like tiny clothes pegs.

"Well done. Let me show you all what we're doing next with these clips," said Penny. She folded the handle as Izzy had told her, and used the clips. "You all do what I'm doing. I want to see who can be really neat in getting these edges lined up like this."

There was much competition around the neatness, to the extent that Penny decided she should invest in some *great job* stickers for future workshops.

"Has anybody here used a sewing machine before?" she asked.

"Me!"

This was more than Penny had hoped for. "What can you tell us all about using a sewing machine safely, er Rose?" asked Penny, reading the girl's sticker.

"Fingers always stay back here," said Rose, rattling her fingernails on the bed of the machine.

"Good rule. Do you think you can work this machine, Rose? If I show you what we're going to sew then you can be the first to have a try. Maybe practise on some scrap."

Rose nodded solemnly and sat at the machine. Penny watched carefully, along with the rest of the group.

Ten minutes later, all of the machines were in action, and Penny had begun to believe that perhaps she could get through this workshop on her own.

"Miss! Miss! It's all got tangled!"

Penny walked over to the machine and saw that there was indeed a jammed-up mess of thread under the needle.

"Try pressing the pedal harder," suggested one of the other children.

Penny held up a hand. "I'm not sure that will —"

There was a whine of protest from the electric motor and then a crunchy bang as something broke.

"Let's turn off the power to this one for a moment," said Penny. She peered in horror at the sewing machine. It looked bad. Surely it was out of action now? "Perhaps we can spread you out to use the other machines?"

"But my bag's stuck in there!" said the girl who had been operating the machine.

"Give me a minute."

Penny went next door. "Izzy!"

"Someone broke a needle, didn't they?" Izzy called. "I can come and sort that out if you open the door."

Penny's hands were on the key, but she paused. "Fine, but if you come back in here, you will pay attention to what I say about safety, yes?"

"I promise."

Penny opened the door and Izzy came out, holding a neatly-constructed flower in her hand. She went into the workshop and presented it to Merida. "What do you think? Will this look nice on your strap?"

"It's lovely!" said Merida. It was a rose, with pink petals and two green leaves peeking out from behind.

"I'll sort out this sewing machine and then we'll sew it on," said Izzy. She sat at the sewing machine that Penny had switched off, and moments later she had loosened the work that was jammed inside. She changed the needle and got it going again.

Penny was able to relax a little when Izzy took charge of the sewing.

The bags were coming along beautifully when Penny remembered something. "Izzy," she whispered, "didn't we say that these bags were going to have their names on?"

"We did say that, yes," said Izzy. "One moment, and I'll show you something." She disappeared into the room next door and came back again. "The machine next door has a built-in alphabet so that it can embroider words. While I was shut up in jail, I made these." She held out a bundle of small plaques, each bearing the name of a child.

"Wow. You made the flower and did all these too?"

"Yep. They can sew them onto their bags once they've finished constructing them."

A little while later, everyone had a bag with their name proudly displayed.

"We need a group picture!" said Penny. "Let's all go and stand outside the front window."

The group assembled outside the recently-painted bay window at the front of the shop. The paintwork gleamed. Penny smiled, confident that the frontage looked as good as it could. She would have to congratulate Aubrey on his excellent work.

Izzy took a group picture of the children holding up their bags, everyone beaming with pride. The different colours and patterns of the bags all reflected the personalities of their creators. Some had embellishments like buttons, bows or buckles. Each was a small work of art, and Penny was thrilled to see them all.

Parents were starting to arrive to collect the children, so Penny steered everyone back inside.

"Before you all go, I need to make sure that we capture your thoughts for future workshops in the ideas book. It's on the counter."

"And look out for your picture in the newspaper!" added Izzy, waving her camera.

Penny kept a careful eye on the attendees who had arrived without paying for a place, so that she could be sure to have a discreet conversation with the adult that came to collect them. She was very keen for the shop to be a well-loved part of the community, but she couldn't afford for it to keep running at a loss.

32

Izzy was a little late to the editorial meeting on Sunday afternoon. The decorative yarn had loosened on her bike. She stopped en route to make some running repairs, mindful that a loose end snarling in the gears could spell disaster.

As she entered, Annalise was showing Tariq and Glenmore photos of the World Book Day event at the library. Free books had been distributed, a local children's writer had come in to do a reading and general book-related fun had been had by all. Nothing was made of the fact that the senior librarian had not been present on account of being dead and in a mortuary somewhere.

Izzy thought best not to ruin the moment by mentioning it.

"Can you forward me those pictures to go in the paper?" she asked.

"I don't have release forms from most of the children. I can definitely send you the one of my Merida. I took it outside our house that morning."

"I still say reading is its own reward," said Glenmore. "We didn't need special book days when we were children."

"Well, possibly true," said Annalise. Izzy's phone pinged with the photo message from her. "Shall we move on to the complaint made by Stuart Dinktrout?" Annalise asked.

"A complaint? What was that?" asked Izzy.

"He has complained that we made Arabella look fat in some of the pictures. Izzy, those were your pictures."

The accusation hung in the air.

"Who is Arabella?" asked Glenmore. "And why is Stuart complaining on her behalf? Seems a bit personal."

Izzy turned over the page. "First of all, Glenmore, Arabella is a pig as you know full well." She held up the page of the Frambeat Gazette so that everyone could see the pictures.

"Ah yes, I remember. Very good pictures, Izzy. The pig is wearing a waistcoat, it's very fetching."

"Yes, she is a delight. I can see that Arabella will be a subject that we can go back to again and again, if we play our cards right. Stuart Dinktrout plans to equip her with a whole wardrobe of outfits and she's got upcoming appearances in lots of shows."

"But these pictures —" started Tariq.

"Oh yes. We need to make sure we get coverage of those events," said Glenmore, nodding decisively.

"We will get coverage, but we must make sure we keep

Stuart Dinktrout happy or he'll reduce our access to Arabella," said Izzy.

"Then you must take better pictures. Perhaps her waistcoat needs buttoning more tightly?" Glenmore suggested.

"No!" Tariq waved his hands in agitation. "These pictures —"

"Does anyone else think it's a little odd that you would want a pig to look slim?" asked Glenmore. "Their normal shape is somewhat tubby, isn't it?"

"There is some controversy about which class of pig she is," said Izzy. "Micro mini or mini micro? Something like that. Dinktrout is in the middle of an argument about it all and if we make Arabella look fat, then it inflames the whole controversy."

"What is wrong with you all?" yelled Tariq. "This is clearly an aspect ratio problem!"

"I will thank you not to shout, young man," said Glenmore. "Now, kindly explain yourself."

Tariq raised his eyes to the ceiling. "I think I have explained this before. In fact, I feel like I have explained it lots of times. The aspect ratio of a picture is the ratio between its height and its width. If you don't keep that ratio consistent then the picture gets stretched."

"I'm sure I don't understand," said Glenmore.

"You made it more wide than you made it tall. It's not difficult. That is why Arabella looks fat in these pictures. It is because they have been stretched widthways."

Glenmore drew himself up haughtily. "Arabella looks fat in these pictures because she is a pig! As a soldiering man, I know when to call a pig a pig. Now, I expect there is a place for your technical gobbledegook in your academic essays or whatnot, but this here is the real world. Isn't that what you came here to experience?"

Tariq's mouth opened and closed wordlessly. Izzy recognised his frustration. He was not the first person to try to explain this concept to Glenmore, but nobody had yet succeeded. He had learned how to use the desktop publishing software and saw it as his duty to cram in maximum content. No arrangement of that content was out of bounds when it came to achieving that goal.

"Yes. Yes, it is," croaked Tariq.

Izzy hoped that he wouldn't bail on them. Quite a lot of their placement students did, once they realised that they were part of a setup that refused to drag its aesthetic into the twenty-first century.

"I have an idea," said Izzy. "Let's offer Stuart a free advert for his petting farm and see if we can win him round."

"Excellent idea, Izzy," said Glenmore. "Annalise, could you talk to Stuart about that idea?"

Annalise nodded.

"Now, who is taking care of the obituaries?" asked Glenmore. "Annalise, perhaps you can work something up for Roy Cotwin and Lorina Reid."

"Are we just doing obituaries?" said Izzy.

"As opposed to what, Izzy?" asked Glenmore.

Izzy wasn't entirely sure what she meant, but thoughts of Lorina's death had unavoidably been fizzing round her head since she — she! Izzy herself — had found the poor woman's body.

"Surely this is front page stuff," she said. "Two unexplained deaths in quick succession. Isn't it our responsibility, as a local newspaper, to look more closely into it all?"

"It was an accident, wasn't it?" said Annalise. "The garden ornament fell off the shelf."

"Then it's worth us at least reporting that much, surely? I mean, it would be a matter for discussion if we wanted to go further than that, but nothing shifts copies like a serial killer story."

"Serial killer?" said Tariq.

"We seem to be jumping to a lot of conclusions there, Izzy," said Glenmore. "It is surely more likely that there is a simple explanation for both of those deaths."

"And I can't imagine that Mr Dinktrout's opinion of us will improve if we're highlighting a death at his garden centre," added Annalise.

"His roses are a cultural feature of the local area," said Glenmore.

"Really?" said Tariq.

"The red and white Dinktrout Rose is a unique variety. The Dinktrout family are listed as the original breeders."

"You can copyright flowers?" said Tariq.

Izzy wasn't sure about this but Annalise was nodding.

"Perhaps what you need is an editorial stance on all this," said Tariq.

Everyone glanced at each other.

"In terms of the deaths," said Tariq, "perhaps you want to make it clear that you're interested in keeping local people safe, so you speculate on some of the possibilities and warn people to take care, making sure they keep their doors and windows locked, that sort of thing. You could run a column on self-defence maybe? You could get hold of a profiler or some other kind of expert and get a quote from them?"

"Interesting," said Glenmore. "What kind of experts do we have access to, everybody?"

The group scrunched up their faces in thought.

"What's the name of that woman with the glamping pods who's an expert in water divining?" offered Annalise.

"Didn't Frank Mountjoy write a pamphlet about farmyard diseases?" said Glenmore.

Tariq held up a hand and pulled a pained expression. "Has anyone got expertise that could be helpful for this story? Maybe medical people?"

"My neighbour does occupational health," said Annalise. "Or we could ask at the medical centre."

"Medical centre it is!" said Glenmore emphatically. "Tariq, why don't you go down there and ask?"

Tariq rolled his eyes. "You know they won't talk to me, right? I need a press pass."

"Now Tariq, we've discussed this. The Gazette is not large enough to qualify for a press pass. You will just have to rely on your personal charm. It's a skill well worth developing in this industry!"

"But —"

"No buts! Tell them you're doing a project for your university, fake an illness and get a quote while they examine you. I don't care what you do, but show some initiative!"

Izzy held up her hand. "Here's a thought. Madame Zelda will be doing horoscopes as usual. Why don't I — I mean she

— find out the star signs of the victims and see if she can work up a story based on that?"

"Good idea," said Glenmore.

Izzy was pleased. This gave her licence to do as she pleased. She could write any piece at all (or write nothing, if it came to that) and justify it to the group. Izzy loved the freedom that the writing of the horoscopes gave her. She believed that it wasn't wrong if she was using her powers for good. Included in Izzy's loose definition of 'good' was anything harmless that brought her personal amusement. She had a sense that exploring two suspicious deaths went beyond that personal amusement and might not be entirely harmless, but when she'd told the team she thought it was their responsibility to explore the situation, she'd meant every word.

"Now, what's this business about you wanting to do an article about people's favourite scissors?" asked Glenmore.

"Fabric scissors. Or shears," said Izzy. "People have them. They're really useful. We asked people to share pictures of them on social media. Even your mum showed off a pink pair the other day, Annalise."

Tariq and Annalise took her phone from her to look.

"But they're just scissors?" said Glenmore, clearly confused.

"Never just scissors. And some people need to treat them with more respect. That Roy Cotwin — God rest his soul — once came into our shop and used my shears without even asking to cut open one of those sealed plastic product packages. Damn near ruined the edge on them."

"Sounds like you're passionate about this topic," said Glenmore.

"I might be," said Izzy.

The old soldier nodded. "Work something up. Let's see if there's room in a future issue."

Izzy saw that Tariq was giving her an oddly suspicious look as he passed her phone back to her.

33

The beginning of a new week rolled round, and Penny had not seen Izzy at all since the Saturday workshop. Things had not ended... brilliantly. Locking your own cousin out of the workshop on account of her lax attitude to child safety was not an ideal state of affairs. Penny felt she ought to apologise, but at the same time she was gripped by the unhelpful notion that she had done absolutely nothing wrong.

Penny saw the free newspaper on the floor. She went over to pick it up and scanned through the local pictures and events. There was always plenty of content, which seemed remarkable, given how small the town was. She ended up at the horoscope page and of course she took a look at Aries.

Family are vital. Don't shut them out. Don't put barriers between you and them. Admit to your failings and accept the wisdom of those closest to you.

"Wow," she said. Even her horoscopes were having a go at her.

She skimmed across the other horoscopes and saw there was indeed a peculiar tone and edge to all of them.

Geminis were advised that disagreements with neighbours were not sufficient cause for physical violence. Capricorns were told that they should bite the bullet and ask out that new person in their life. Aquariuses were given the sage advice to admit what they'd done and atone for their sins. Most oddly of all, Libras were informed that a deep plum purple would be the ideal colour for a new umbrella.

Penny looked at the by-line. Horoscopes by Madame Zelda. She wondered how much of a living Madame Zelda could be making, dishing out brolly-related fortunes.

The doorbell jangled, and it wasn't Izzy coming in with morning coffees and breakfast food. Not that Izzy was required to bring in drink and food. Penny just wanted to see her cousin and make sure that the weekend's craziness had not created a weird rift between them. But it was not Izzy, it was Aubrey the painter.

Penny's involuntary disappointment did not go unnoticed.

"Not pleased to see me?" he said.

"Just wondering where Izzy was."

"I doubt she's got lost on the way to work," he said gently.

"No, I..." She shook herself and applied a mental reset. "Good morning! How very nice to see you. Have you come to browse our wares?"

He grinned. "I came in to see if you'd looked at that quote I sent you." It was his turn to look awkward and hesitate. "I mean, I'm also just popping in and saying hi. If you're not rushed off your feet."

She looked about the entirely empty shop. "I think things are tolerably quiet for the time being. I thought *you* were rushed off your feet this week."

Aubrey angled a shoulder. "I've been told to stop work on repainting Roy's house. Solicitors have had words."

"It did seem Stuart was a bit too keen to get that repainted. Unseemly, even."

"He's a man who makes decisions and sticks with them."

"Doesn't like people going against his wishes?" she asked, recalling the rancour in the cryptic argument she'd heard between Stuart and Lorina shortly before she'd died.

"He is a force to be reckoned with within the town," Aubrey agreed. "The Dinktrout Rose has been a feature of the local business scene for decades. But even the mighty Stuart Dinktrout has to pay attention to threatening letters from legal bods." He clapped his hands together. "Which does mean I could start work on the interior decorating here, if you're interested."

Penny pulled a face. She'd looked at the quote. It was perfectly reasonable and the workshop spaces definitely needed more than a lick of paint.

"We'll do the workshop and shop space, but not extend to the upstairs living spaces if that's all right with you," she said.

"You're the customer," he said merrily. "Don't want to make changes to that charming apartment space?"

"Don't know how long I'll be staying," she replied. "Not even sure if Izzy appreciates my involvement."

He laughed. "Are you kidding me? I think she loves having you here."

Penny drew back, frowning. "Really?"

"It's..." Aubrey waved his hands in the air in front of him, as though trying to capture words like they were butterflies. "It's like Izzy is a bouncing puppy or a... a circus clown. She's full of this energy, these creative juices and she wants to go off and do everything under the sun."

"Sounds like our Izzy."

"But a puppy left to its own devices is going to be very unhappy. Someone needs to feed it. Someone needs to patch up the fence around the garden so it doesn't run out and head into traffic."

"Izzy's going to get hit by a car?"

Aubrey shook his head. "It's all well and good being a circus clown but someone still needs to sell tickets and popcorn."

"And I'm the tickets and popcorn woman."

"The ringmaster."

Penny thought on that. "Ringmaster and clown, huh?"

"Could be a winning combination," he said.

She stroked her chin. Maybe she and Izzy did complement one another. That still didn't explain why Izzy was late for work.

34

Izzy had spent the early morning retracing what she imagined was Lorina's final journey up to Dinktrout's.

She wanted to experience the walk in the same way Lorina might have done on that fateful trip. She told nobody about her intentions, because she could already hear phrases like 'leave the sleuthing to the police' and 'are you out of your mind, Izzy?' ringing in her ears.

The fact that the Frambeat Gazette editorial team were so willing to accept that Lorina's death was a mere accident did not sit well with her. Two unexplained deaths in the town within a week of one another seemed most peculiar.

Lorina's final journey had started at the library, so Izzy had gone there first and walked past St Michael's church. She had wondered if Lorina had relatives buried in the churchyard. If so, that was the sort of thing that would have been on her mind if she'd come this way. It was natural to murmur a fond greeting to a deceased relative. Izzy had nominated a grave and given it a nod as she passed.

She had then carried on along the narrow street. Did Lorina enjoy the squeezed-up closeness of these brightly painted houses? It was familiar and charming. Izzy imagined the houses on either side of the street leaning in to share a joke. Past the castle, she turned onto the junction that would take her away from the town centre. She turned down the Badingham Road and walked away to greener spaces.

Would Lorina have grumbled about some of the newer houses that had popped up on the outskirts of town? Even traditionalists must acknowledge that people needed houses.

Izzy was warming up now. She'd been walking for long enough that she was feeling hot under her coat. Lorina would have been the same, of course, in her Alice in Wonderland dress. She'd regret the extra layer of the apron. How fit was she? Did Lorina do yoga or go to the gym?

So many questions! Was Izzy learning anything at all or simply acknowledging that she and Penny didn't really know much about Lorina?

A little under a mile later, she reached the garden centre. Gravel crunched under her feet as she crossed the car park.

A moment of guilt passed over her. She was returning to the scene of the woman's death. This was not simple morbid curiosity. She was actively showing an interest in an untimely death.

Why are you doing this? asked a little voice in her head and, promptly, Izzy felt as if she were being interviewed by a news reporter on the telly.

I want to know how Lorina died, she told him in her most formal TV voice.

Why is that important, Izzy? he asked.

Um, she was a valued customer. She died in one of our dresses.

And that makes it your responsibility?

No, Colin, it doesn't make it my responsibility, she said defensively. *But I was the first one to find the body, and Penny and I had been talking about her and had even thought she was behind Roy Cotwin's death.*

For our viewers at home, Roy was the man found dead of poisoning outside his own house last week, said the imaginary reporter, who was now, apparently, called Colin.

That's right, Colin, she said. *People had their reasons for hating Roy and it seems Lorina wasn't afraid to rub people up the wrong way either.*

You think she was murdered, Izzy?

I just want to retrace her steps and look at the flamingos, Colin. I just want to look at the flamingos.

She waved the imaginary reporter away with a silent, *no more comment,* and to the pops of a dozen entirely fictitious camera flashes, she went inside.

Izzy instinctively felt it was important she looked like a regular customer, and not some sort of ghoul hanging around at the scene of Lorina's death.

She browsed packets of seeds. Sunflowers were easy to grow, weren't they? She picked up a packet and wandered further in. Dinktrout's had space in the car park for coaches, and Izzy had seen them turn up before. A coach full of seniors would arrive, and they would have lunch in the restaurant and spend most of a day browsing the displays and buying plants. She had no idea where they came from, but it was a winning formula for Stuart Dinktrout. Captive pensioners spending the entire day in the same place must be quite valuable, although right now they were in Izzy's way as she tried to get to the display that she was really interested in.

"You will see that all of these ornaments are now located on the floor rather than on the racking up there," a coach driver was saying to the visitors gathered round. "Obviously it's not for me to speculate, but that will be a health and safety response to the unfortunate death of a customer very recently."

"Is that where she died?" asked an old geezer in a beige anorak.

"Indeed. It appears that she was struck on the head by a flamingo ornament falling from the rack, even though it appears to be secure. Some people have suggested that the ghost of a seventeenth century witch might be responsible, but of course I could not possibly comment. If these flamingos could talk, what would they tell us, eh?"

The coach driver had his cap pushed back and his audience was fixated on his lurid tale. Izzy watched as the last remaining metal flamingos were seized and put into shopping trolleys.

When she eventually got through to the display, there was not a single flamingo left.

"Bugger."

Izzy wanted a flamingo. She hadn't realised she wanted one but now, faced with the scene and the method of Lorina's death, she grasped that her investigation demanded one.

There was nothing else for it. She followed the group. They were dispersing slightly, small gaggles of friends sticking together in ever-shrinking groups. It would be easier to target a loner if she was going to steal their flamingo. Strictly speaking it wasn't stealing as they hadn't yet paid for it. Izzy followed the white-haired bloke in the anorak into the tools section. She watched as he studied all of the hand tools in forensic detail, holding them, testing their weight and their balance and examining the labels. Izzy hung back, waiting for him to turn away from his trolley for a good few seconds. He pulled out his phone and she drew nearer, hopeful that this was her moment.

"Hello darling! Yes, I'm just looking at the tools now. I'm having a tough time deciding so I thought I'd give you a call. If you had to decide between easy-grip and lightweight, which would suit your aunt best? I'm thinking the grip thing since the stroke, am I right?"

Izzy eased herself into range, pretending to look at kneeling pads.

"Very good. Yes, you're right. I got her a surprise, too. A decorative feature that she can have by the door. It's shiny and it's got a story. She's going to love it!"

Izzy's hand was already around the flamingo's neck, but as she heard the man talking she relaxed her grip. She couldn't take this. Snatching a present for a stroke victim definitely wasn't who she was. She took a step back, turned and melted away. She would need a back-up plan.

Izzy approached the customer service desk. "Can I please get one of the flamingos? Like you've got outside? Maybe you have some stock that's not out yet?"

The woman gave her a cool look. "All gone? Tut. Vultures."

"Fairly certain they're flamingos."

"People wanting to buy one of those things that killed her." Her cool gaze became even cooler.

"I'm not a vulture," said Izzy. "I just wanted a flamingo." She didn't add that she wanted it to test how probable it was that Lorina had been killed by an accidentally falling ornament. "Maybe you could order one for me?" she suggested.

35

P enny heard the jingle of the shop door while she was upstairs with Aubrey. She'd just made him a cup of tea, and the two of them were looking at colour charts of paints.

"Hang on! Coming down!" she called to the potential customer and headed for the stairs.

"It's just me," Izzy called back up.

Penny hurried down nonetheless. There was Izzy in the shop, looking red in the face and somewhat sweaty.

"I wondered where you'd got to," said Penny.

"Sorry, I'm late."

"I was worried."

"Really?" said Izzy.

"I... I thought I'd upset you."

Izzy's red face frowned. "Why?"

"I did lock you in a room on Saturday."

Izzy blinked at her. "You did. It happens."

"What?"

"Nanna Lem once tied me to a chair to stop me getting over-excited with the Christmas tree decorations."

"She tied you up when you were a child?" said Penny, disbelieving.

"No, this was last year. There's just something about tinsel that brings out the wild abandon in me."

"Um. Okay," said Penny, making a mental note to be a long way from Izzy when Christmas came round. "Anyway, sorry."

Izzy shrugged like it was nothing. There was a creak from upstairs. Izzy looked at Penny.

"Burglars?"

"It's just Aubrey," said Penny and then, as a grin spread across Izzy's face, she waved her hands firmly in denial. "He's come round to see what needs doing."

The grin did not go away.

"He's a painter!" said Penny.

"Big dextrous hands," said Izzy.

"Stop it. Come up and offer an opinion."

Feeling the embarrassment flush her cheeks, Penny led the way back upstairs to the workshop area.

Aubrey had found something balled up by the skirting boards. It was one of the tote bags from the workshop at the weekend.

"That's Merida's," said Penny. "She decorated hers with *Frozen* star shapes."

Izzy straightened it out. "She must have forgotten it. I'll take it back to her later."

Aubrey gestured at Izzy's crazy mood board hanging on the calico partition.

"Some really interesting ideas here," he said.

Penny wasn't sure if Aubrey was just being polite. To Penny's eyes, the mood board appeared to be a chaotic collection of astrological symbols, celebrity photos and splodgy finger paints.

"I particularly like the contrast of the creams and the pink here," he added.

"I'm taking my inspiration from the signs of the zodiac," said Izzy.

"I'm a Capricorn myself," Aubrey told her.

"Oh, I'm well aware of that," said Izzy in a tone that struck Penny as weirdly knowing.

Aubrey held out the colour charts in his hands for them both to look at. "Further thoughts? If we settle on a colour today, I can probably get it in before the end of the week."

"I do like the blue," said Penny.

"That was Lorina's favourite colour," said Izzy.

Penny frowned. "I'm not sure I want to pick a colour just because it was a dead woman's favourite."

"It would be a nice tribute to a murdered woman," said Izzy.

"Murdered?" asked Aubrey.

"Maybe," said Izzy.

"It's a possibility," said Penny. "A vague, vague possibility."

"I thought people said it was an accident," said Aubrey.

"We'll see," replied Izzy.

"We don't know if anyone would want to murder her," said Penny.

Aubrey shrugged. "Well, when it comes to murder, you always have to ask yourself one question."

"What's that?"

"Who benefits?" he said.

"Like in the will, you mean?" asked Izzy.

"Maybe," said Aubrey. "But what do I know? I'm just a painter and decorator."

36

P enny waved a thanks to the postman.

There were a number of delivery drivers who dropped stuff off at the shop. Despite seeming to have very few customers, Nanna Lem was still apparently keen to get new stock in. The delivery guys would occasionally stay for a drink and always enjoyed a chat, which was why Penny found it surprising to spot a parcel outside the door as the postman left. It was especially disturbing as it looked like a huge brown chrysalis, four feet tall, with something weird and metallic emerging from torn segments, like a robot butterfly.

"Oh hey, did you leave that?" she called to the postman.

He looked at her. "No. I would have brought it inside, obviously."

She turned to the mystery package, propped outside the door. It leaned against the woodwork, as if it had been left there deliberately. She leaned down, looking for a label.

There was writing scrawled across the brown paper. It was partially torn away, but Penny thought that it said: *Izzy / sewing shop*

Was it a delivery address? Was it a veiled threat?

She reached out a hand to the package. Brown paper swaddled it very lightly, but it fell away at the slightest touch. A large piece flopped down from the top. A beady rivet eye stared at Penny, and she realised that she was looking at a flamingo garden ornament.

"Oh, my!" she breathed, feeling a chill run through her.

It really wouldn't do to have such a macabre thing sitting around outside the shop. It was very early on a Tuesday morning and there was not yet much movement in the marketplace. Penny crouched to pick it up, was momentarily surprised by its weight, and then brought it inside.

She set it down in the centre of the shop and, with a sense of morbid curiosity, unwrapped it. She stepped back and regarded the flamingo. She'd seen ornaments in this style before. Sheets and rods of iron were welded together to create an impressionistic shape of a thing. The welding spots were almost deliberately messy and the metal was burnished to a colourful sheen. The effect was attractive but there was something wilfully industrial about it. What was the word? Steampunk. It was a steampunk flamingo.

"And someone killed Lorina with you," she said to no one at all.

With a start, she realised she was being watched. Old McGillicuddy and Timmy, the man and his dog (she couldn't recall which was which), stood outside the shop window, looking at her as she conversed with a motionless killer flamingo.

"It's not my flamingo," she called.

The old man looked horrified, and he and his dog moved on.

37

Izzy had arrived at the shop to find Aubrey bringing in dustcloths and paints to begin work on the workshop space, and to find Penny in a state of great agitation because a flamingo had turned up outside. Izzy had talked her down from the notion that it was a sinister gift from a murderer, and had been truthful about the fact that she had ordered it for herself from Dinktrout Nurseries.

"What on earth do you want that for?" asked Penny.

"Things," said Izzy evasively.

"What things?"

"Maybe we could use it as part of a window display?" said Izzy. She wasn't quite ready to tell Penny that she wanted to test out murder theories.

"Why would we want a killer flamingo as part of a window display? Hey, folks! You remember that woman who got killed by a flamingo? Come see ours."

"It's just an idea."

"You're always full of ideas," said Penny doubtfully, and went to check on Aubrey.

Izzy left the flamingo casually wrapped at the top of the stairs until lunch time, then snatched it up while Penny was washing her hands. With a hasty shouted goodbye, she was out of the door and jogging across to the Co-op before Penny could respond.

She tucked the flamingo under her arm and went inside, scouting along the fruit and veg.

"Oh hi, excuse me. Do you have a watermelon?" she asked.

"We have melon segments in the chiller section."

"I needed a whole one."

The chap shook his head. "We don't often have them, in to be honest. When we do, they sometimes go off because they aren't that popular."

"Well what else do you have that's similar?" Izzy asked.

"Similar in what way?"

Izzy paused for a moment. It would not be a good idea to share her thinking at this point. That would mean saying something like 'similar to a human head.' "Oh, I was after something big and juicy." Izzy heard the words coming out of her mouth and realised that in an effort not to sound criminally weird, she had ended up sounding flirtatiously weird.

"I see."

This was bad. She needed to clarify. "When I say juicy, I really mean squishy. Something with a bit of give." Izzy clamped down on the words before any more could escape. Nothing she could say was going to make this any better.

"What you really want then is a slightly rotten watermelon. Got one of them out back."

Izzy was taken aback. Maybe the store assistant had guessed what she was doing? "Er yes! Actually, that would work well."

"I'll go get it. I can label it up for 10p."

Izzy was about to argue that surely it should be free if they were going to throw it away, but she managed to stop herself. Probably it was a till thing. She nodded gratefully.

A few minutes later she was walking away with her flamingo under one arm and a watermelon with a large bruise under the other.

She had decided to conduct her experiment at the castle. Framlingham castle might seem an odd place to conduct a murder reconstruction, but it was midweek in early March and there were very few tourists about.

Framlingham Castle was a massive twelfth century fortress of a castle, overlooking the boggy Framlingham mere and five minutes' walk from the shop. Although many of the castle walls were crumbling, there was a high walkway around the top that the braver visitors could take. The walls were surrounded by a deep grassy valley around the outer edge of the castle.

This would give her the opportunity to simulate the flamingo falling from height. Izzy trotted down the side and put the watermelon at the base of the valley, and then climbed back up with the flamingo. She waited a moment to make sure no other people were around and then she pulled out her phone so that she could record the experiment.

She reckoned her flamingo was at least twice as high up

as any of the displays at Dinktrouts. She held it at arm's length and started the video. She dropped the flamingo over the slope and onto the melon. It missed.

"Blast!"

She went down to the bottom again. The flamingo body had separated from its legs. As she climbed back up to the bridge, Izzy pushed them back into place and tried to squish the metal so that they would stay there. The flamingo looked a little deformed by its experience, but it held together. She set herself up again, and this time her positioning was more accurate. The flamingo dropped onto the watermelon and glanced off.

"Huh."

It certainly hadn't smashed into a pulverised mess. She went down to investigate. The flamingo had struck it on the rotten side, and hadn't even punctured the skin.

"CSI Framlingham," she pronounced in gravelly voiceover style. "The victim's wounds were not sustained due to the impact of a falling flamingo."

There was a very obvious follow-up experiment to be done, and Izzy looked around again to make sure she was alone.

"Mr Flamingo, I am sorry, but this is for science." She picked him up by his slightly wobbly legs and whacked his head down onto the watermelon.

This time it did get squished. Izzy plucked the flamingo out of the sticky juice and then regarded the watermelon. She took some pictures and then realised how messy she was going to get trying to remove the remains of her experiment.

She scrambled up the side, and found a bin on the way

out of the castle grounds in which she could dump the remainder of the melon.

As she turned onto Church Street, the woman adjusting the prices on the outdoor board of the ice cream shop gave her and her flamingo a funny look.

"Just me and my flamingo going for a walk," Izzy told her.

"What's that pink stuff on it?" asked the woman.

"The victim's brains," said Izzy. She had been aiming for a light and goofy tone but she realised immediately that it had come across as weird and tasteless. "Obviously, not the real victim's brains," she added hurriedly.

"You're disgusting," said the woman.

"I'm sure it will wash off," said Izzy but the woman had hurried inside and shut the door.

38

Izzy got more than a few suspicious looks and comments on the short journey back to the Cozy Crafts shop, and was beginning to see Penny's point about the morbid nature of the ornament.

Penny looked at her when she re-entered. "What have you been doing?"

"Honestly," said Izzy. "It was a good and valid scientific experiment. I think I'd best put this somewhere else, though. Out of sight maybe."

"A good idea," said Penny.

Izzy tucked it away at the foot of the stairs, well out of sight of the main shop. Merida's tote bag was laid out on the counter.

"We should run more workshops," said Penny. "They could be an absolute lifeline for this shop."

"World Book Day only comes once a year," said Izzy.

"It's nearly spring. There's Easter coming up."

"Stitch your own egg-collecting pouch."

"Exactly."

"I reckon we could do sewing birthday parties too."

"Is that a thing?" asked Penny.

"It is if we make it a thing. We could give away some of the fancy dress stuff that never sells. We have a ton of unconvincing masks."

"We do indeed. Some of them are terrifying."

"A lot of Halloween masks."

"I meant the cutesy animal masks. Those dead eyes."

"We've got other events coming up through the year," said Izzy. "They put stuff on at the castle." Izzy took her phone out to look at her calendar. Since the Frambeat Gazette wanted its finger on the pulse of events in the town, she had a list of them on her phone. "The Fram classic car weekend is in July time, I think and..."

A message had come through on her phone.

"Tariq wants to see us in the café down the road at five," she said.

"Tariq?"

"Student helper on the Frambeat Gazette. Nice enough fellow."

"If you want to go off at five, I'm sure I can handle things here."

"Us," said Izzy. "He specifically wants to see you, too. He says it's important."

Izzy held out the phone to Penny's frowning face to show her. There was a sudden metallic clang, a yell of alarm and a heavy thump.

They dashed to the bottom of the stairs where they found

Aubrey sat awkwardly, his legs tangled with those of the metal flamingo and most of the contents of a tin of paint over both man and flamingo. The paint was the light pink they were intending to use for much of the workshop woodwork.

"Oh, no!" said Penny and rushed to help him.

"Didn't see the damn thing," he muttered, pulling himself up.

Penny flung an irritated hand out at the flamingo. "Get that thing out of here, Izzy. It's cursed, I'm sure."

"It's not the actual one that killed —"

"Izzy! Just do it!"

Izzy picked up the flamingo and, holding it carefully so the paint that covered its head, neck and body didn't drip any further, whisked it away through the shop and put it on the pavement immediately outside where it could cause no further harm.

When she got back inside, Penny was sponging paint from Aubrey's overalls with a towel.

"It's a nice pink, though," said Izzy as she passed.

39

O nce the shop was cleaned and Aubrey had been sent home to change and the business of the day concluded, Penny and Izzy shut up shop and walked down to the café at the bottom of Bridge Street. Their route took them past the library, over the shallow river that ran through the town and past a block of sheltered accommodation flats. The café had an area of Parisian-style chairs and tables outside, but it was probably too early in the year for anyone to want to sit there.

Lights were on inside the café. A slender man, at least five years younger than Penny herself, sat at a table in the corner.

"Tariq, Penny. Penny, Tariq," said Izzy.

Young Tariq had his fingertips resting lightly around a hot drink in a take-out cup.

"They're shutting up soon but they can probably do you a drink. On me," he added.

"We're good," said Penny.

"Actually, I like the look of that jam sponge," said Izzy.

She glanced at the woman behind the counter, nodded silently, and a slice of cake was served from beneath the elegant glass cloche.

"Always interested in receiving a mysterious summons from a stranger," said Penny, taking a seat opposite Tariq.

"You're probably wondering why I've gathered you here," he said.

"Yes, that's kind of what I meant."

"I know, but that's what you have to say in these situations. 'You're probably wondering why I've gathered you here.'"

"Is it?" asked Penny.

"It's called the 'parlour scene'."

Izzy, sitting down with cake in hand, looked around. "Fairly sure it's a café."

Tariq looked a bit uncomfortable, a little nervous. "Maybe I should get straight to the point."

"If you like," said Penny supportively.

He looked from one to the other and then back again, and finally said, "I know you killed Roy Cotwin and Lorina Reid."

A laugh burst out of Penny. Izzy paused with a piece of cake on her fork.

"You what?" said Penny.

"You murdered them," he repeated. "Either together or individually."

"Cor," said Izzy. "This is an unexpected twist."

"Twist?" said Penny. "It's ludicrous."

"We had our own list of suspects lined up, but we never thought to add ourselves."

"Please tell me this is all a massive joke," said Penny.

"No, this is very serious indeed," said Tariq. "I wouldn't have given it much thought if Izzy hadn't tried to bring it up repeatedly at the newspaper editorial meeting. Killers and their need to return to the scene of the crime, both physically and mentally. It's a genuine thing."

"And you think we did it?" asked Penny, incredulous.

"The evidence is strong," said Tariq.

"So, we poisoned Roy Cotwin."

He nodded. "Rat poison in an old glass bottle he drank from at the library."

"No, no, no. We thought that too, which was why I went back to collect it," said Penny.

"Yes. A member of the public saw you doing that and overheard the conversation. The same member of the public overheard you phoning an anonymous tip-off to the police, with a claim that the fatal rat poison was being stored at the library."

"Which member of the public?"

"A journalist doesn't reveal their sources."

"So, you think we poisoned Roy?" said Penny, irritated. "Why? I'd only met him that day. I don't just rock up in town and start murdering people."

"Yes," said Tariq smoothly, fixing her with what she assumed he thought was a perceptive gaze. He was definitely savouring the murder detective role. "How odd it is that you arrive in Fram, a pleasant rural town, and within a week, two people have been murdered."

"That's something-something logical. I forget what it's called but just because A follows B, doesn't mean that A caused B."

"A being Penny turning up and B being two horrible murders," offered Izzy helpfully.

"We just don't have a motive," said Penny.

Tariq smiled. He was clearly enjoying this, a little too much for Penny's taste. "I struggled with that too. Until you," he turned abruptly from Penny to Izzy, grimaced, and rubbed his neck before continuing. "Until you started showing pictures of your favourite scissors at the meeting and revealed, quite tellingly, that Roy had used *your* fabric scissors to cut open a plastic package in your shop. You admitted that the topic aroused great passions within you."

"Not enough to kill a man, though."

Tariq cocked an eyebrow. Penny suspected he had been practising it in a mirror. "Did you not until recently have a note pinned up in your shop listing 'legitimate reasons' for murdering customers?"

"That was just Nanna Lem's joke."

"Which you took down."

"I took it down when I took control of the shop," said Penny, "on account of it being tasteless."

"And incriminating," said Tariq.

"This is flimsy stuff to be honest, Tariq."

"Really? Because when Izzy gave me her phone to look at the pictures of fabric scissors, I took the opportunity to look at her internet browsing history."

"That was cheeky," said Izzy.

"Apart from the surprising number of searches for

'squirrels in hats', I couldn't help but be intrigued by searches for 'rat poison suicide' and 'how quickly does rat poison kill a person?'"

Izzy looked guiltily at Penny. "I did say I'd done some research."

"*After* Roy's death," Penny pointed out. "And there *was* rat poison in the library kitchen. I looked."

"An odd thing to be looking for," said Tariq. "And the police didn't find anything."

"Maybe if you tell us who that member of the public was, we could find out who knew that I knew, eh?"

"You're trying to throw the spotlight of suspicion away from yourselves."

"Because we didn't do it!" said Penny.

"I certainly didn't do it," said Izzy.

Penny glared at her. "Are you saying I did?"

"Of course not. I'm just saying I didn't."

"By which you're implying that I did."

"No, I'm just being logical."

Penny scoffed. "Well, I guess there's a first time for everything!"

"I am not saying I think you did it."

"I am," said Tariq. "For whatever reason, perhaps deeper and more valid than those I've uncovered so far, you decided to do away with Roy Cotwin."

"And we killed Lorina too, did we?" said Penny, scathingly. "Just after we sold her that lovely Alice in Wonderland dress?"

"I doubt you would have killed her before you had

received payment. How much would she pay for a dress like that?"

Izzy opened her mouth, but Penny put up a hand to stop her.

"Don't give him more ammunition to use against us, pathetically tenuous though it might be."

"I don't think he's got any evidence that we killed Lorina," said Izzy.

"Although you were there when she died, Izzy," Tariq pointed out.

"I what?"

"You were the first person on the scene at her death. Suspicious that you would be the one to find her."

"Someone has to be the first person find a body," said Penny.

"I was following a rabbit," added Izzy.

"See, she was —" Penny stopped and looked at her cousin. "You were what?"

"I was following a little white rabbit. His name is Percy."

"You didn't tell me that before."

"It didn't seem pertinent."

"It seems the kind of fact that you'd mention."

"It's not a very plausible excuse," said Tariq.

"It's not an excuse! It's what happened," said Izzy.

"You can tell that to the jury. And I don't suppose you have an alibi for the time of the actual murder which was — what? — five minutes before you found the body."

"I was with Arabella."

"Arabella."

"A pig," said Penny.

"Yes, she's a pig," confirmed Izzy.

Tariq shook his head slowly. "Pigs. Rabbits. They can hardly be called to testify in court."

"I've just made Arabella a waistcoat. She'd look good in the witness box."

"You're not helping," said Penny. "So, Tariq, why did we kill Lorina? Did she misuse our shears too? Did she bend one of our needles?"

"I can only guess that she knew about Roy's death. Perhaps you needed to silence her."

"So, no motive at all then, really?"

"I don't have all the pieces," he admitted, "but then there's the matter of the flamingo."

"Flamingo?" said Izzy innocently.

"You were seen with one about town today. You were up at the castle. Trying to dump it, perhaps?"

"We don't deny that there is a flamingo ornament similar to the one that accidentally killed Lorina in our possession," said Penny.

"Not accidentally," said Izzy.

"What?"

"Not accidentally. I did some tests. Those things are heavy but they'd barely give you a headache if one dropped on you. You'd need to swing it with a bit of clout."

"You've been practising," said Tariq.

"On a melon," said Izzy.

Penny looked to Tariq. "Honestly, sometimes I just don't understand the things she says. Rabbits. Melons. She lives in a slightly different reality to the rest of us."

"And I could not help but notice that you repainted the flamingo earlier today," said Tariq.

"We didn't repaint it," said Penny.

"Not deliberately," said Izzy. "That was Aubrey."

"The painter and decorator," said Tariq. "The one who was seen having a loud argument with a solicitor about the painting of Roy Cotwin's house."

"I wouldn't call it a loud argument," said Izzy.

"You were there?" asked Penny.

"Oh, it seems like you two are everywhere when it comes to this sordid business," said Tariq.

"It's a small town," replied Penny.

"And the truth will come out," he said. "Roy Cotwin abused your beloved fabric scissors so you poisoned him. You removed the fatal bottle, took down the incriminating note in the shop and gave false information to the police to throw them off the scent. When you realised Lorina somehow knew about it, you waited until you had the money for the dress and then followed her up to the garden centre. You picked up a metal flamingo and — clonk! — off with her head before slipping away with some cockamamie alibi featuring rabbits and pigs. You then attempted to hide the murder weapon beneath a fresh coat of paint and assumed you had got away with it all."

Penny and Izzy stared at him.

"That's the most unbelievable load of nonsense I've ever heard," said Penny.

"I can't believe that you actually used the word 'cockamamie' in a sentence," said Izzy.

"Believe what you want, say what you want," said Tariq.

"Those are the facts. I will be writing them up, and if the Frambeat Gazette won't publish my exposé then I'll simply forward it to the police."

He stood and nodded politely to them. "Ladies," he said, and left.

Penny and Izzy looked at each other. The woman at the counter looked at them too.

"Oh, don't mind me," said the woman when she saw Penny looking back at her. "I just serves cakes and toasties."

40

Penny and Izzy convened an emergency meeting that evening. And because emergencies required energy they bought hot tuna and cheese toasties and extra cake from the café before it closed for the night.

They sat in Penny's room — Penny in the tall green armchair, Izzy in the squat purple one — and munched fretfully on their evening meal.

"This is very bad news," said Penny.

"Speaking as part of the editing team, I don't think the Frambeat Gazette will print Tariq's wild accusations," said Izzy.

"Does it matter?" asked Penny, wiping her cheese-greased fingers on a napkin. "One way or another, he's going to share his story."

"Do you think the police are going to take us in for questioning?"

"God, I hope not," said Penny.

"Don't think you'll cope well with prison life?"

"We're not going to go to prison, Izzy, but if word gets round, if we're even invited to Woodbridge police station for questioning, then that's going to do our reputation a world of damage."

"Not sure I've got much of a reputation in the first place," said Izzy.

"Of course, you have. This shop has a reputation. We were building a new one. Dressmaking, workshops, it was all very slowly coming together. And as for me... no matter what you say, I'm an outsider. I'll never be accepted if they think I'm a killer."

"Then what shall we do?"

Penny straightened up in her chair. "We're going to have to find the answer to this mystery ourselves."

"We are?" said Izzy, her eyes sparkling in the room's warm yellow light.

"And, to be clear, we are in this situation mostly because of you."

"Me?"

"Oh, yes. Chasing after rabbits and suspiciously buying flamingo ornaments and googling how to murder people."

"I'm not the one who's been sneaking around the library, removing bottles from displays and searching for rat poison."

"Hmmm." She had a point there, although Penny still felt the weight of responsibility fell more heavily on Izzy.

"And how do we solve this?"

"We look at our suspects and our clues, I guess," said Penny. "I've not actually had to solve many murders before."

"If murders they are. Let me get my notebook." Izzy

jumped up and out of the room. She returned with a large sketchbook. There were little plastic diamonds and glitter on the cover, and stick-on letters that spelled out 'My fashion designs'. Penny had selected a small iced bun from the cake selection and was trying to eat it without getting icing all over her fingers.

"Suspects, then," she began. "If we assume that Roy was indeed murdered at Lorina's retirement drinks then there were four suspects there: Stuart Dinktrout, Pam Ockenden, her daughter Annalise, and Lorina."

"Lorina is a victim," said Izzy.

"But it's possible that she killed Roy and then someone else killed her."

"You were there, too."

"But we know I didn't do it. *I* know I didn't do it."

"Also Annalise's daughter, Pam's granddaughter, Merida, was there."

"Are we going to start accusing a ten-year-old girl?" said Penny.

Izzy sucked thoughtfully on the end on her pen. "I doubt she could swing the flamingo murder weapon with the necessary force."

"So, four suspects," said Penny, "three of whom might also be responsible for Lorina's death."

Izzy started to write the names on the page.

"My money is on Stuart Dinktrout," she said. "He's very protective of the town. He positively burned with the need to repaint Roy's ugly house."

"And we know there was something odd going on between him and Lorina. She knew something that could ruin him. That's what he said." She closed her eyes as she tried to remember. "He said she had to give him the picture. So we're talking about photographic evidence of some sort."

"He's a man with a lot to lose," Izzy added. "Dinktrout Nurseries is a big business, as is the Dinktrout Rose. A business empire and no one to share it with, apart from a pig."

"Never married."

"Engaged but never married. If he did it to protect his fortune, then his motive for killing Lorina is sound. And she did die in his garden centre when she was on her way to see him."

"But an ugly painted house is not a great motive for killing Roy. It strikes me that the people with the best motives for killing Roy are Annalise and Pam."

"I've known Annalise a long time and I think she's too nice to kill someone."

"I suspect they've said that about a lot of murderers," said Penny. "Roy was a slimy creep of a man, an unpleasant predator. Annalise might have poisoned him to stop him harassing her."

"Pam might have done it to protect her daughter from him."

"We must consider that the perpetrator might not have actually intended to kill him. A bit of poison to put him out of action for a few days, to teach him a lesson. Maybe they didn't know rat poison would kill him."

Izzy continued to make notes. "I get the impression that Lorina was not an easy woman to work with. A bit brusque."

"A bit of a bully," Penny conceded. "Her zeal for literature rather than anything TV or movie related was probably excessive."

"I heard she gave young Merida abuse for turning up to a previous World Book Day event dressed as Elsa from *Frozen*."

"Oh, having their child picked on will bring out the vengeful nature in any mother or grandmother," said Penny with conviction.

"And finally, Lorina. Who couldn't have committed her own murder, obviously, but had good reasons to despise Roy."

Penny nodded. "He was a bully to her in the workplace and probably forced her to take retirement. Maybe she had been defrauding the library out of money. Who knows? It seems reasonable that a woman who was blackmailing Stuart could also be capable of stealing from her employer."

"Four suspects, then," said Izzy and showed Penny her clear notes over a two-page spread.

"And now we must look for clues," said Penny. She felt far less certain about this part. They weren't police detectives. They couldn't do DNA tests and fingerprinting or haul people in for questioning. They simply had to rely on what was available right in front of them.

"When Lorina died, she had a bunch of books with her," said Izzy. "Local history books."

"She and Stuart were arguing in the local history section," said Penny, "and Lorina was dead keen for me to take out a book of history photos."

"Pictures," said Izzy thoughtfully. "We did a profile on Stuart Dinktrout in the Frambeat Gazette. Lots of background information on him there. Annalise makes sure all back copies are stored among the periodicals at the library."

"Excellent. Some local history research beckons."

"I could pop round to Annalise's with Merida's tote bag and ask some subtle questions. If Annalise is working, Pam might be there."

"Are you capable of asking subtle questions?" Penny said, doubtfully.

"Of course I am."

Penny didn't feel confident this was the case, but chose to say nothing.

"So, I think you should go to the library and check out the history books and the Frambeat back issues," said Izzy. "If Annalise is there, you can question her too."

"Meanwhile, you will go and visit Pam and be super subtle."

"Super subtle," Izzy nodded. "Oh, and maybe I could have a word with Madame Zelda and ask her to make some pointed horoscope predictions for our suspects, see if it pricks their consciences."

"Hasn't she already done that?" asked Penny, with a wry smile.

"Has she?"

Penny licked the last of the icing off her fingertips. "I know Madame Zelda is you, Izzy."

"Don't know what you're talking about."

"Telling me to not be so fussy about rules. Telling poor Aubrey to ask me out. I'm not daft. I think you've got a big book with a whole load of people's birthdays in it and you use those horoscopes to tell people what you want them to hear."

"You don't want Aubrey to ask you out?"

Penny gave her a stern, if puzzled look. "I don't know how long I'm in Fram for and maybe I haven't got time in my life for romance."

"Romance. You sound so old fashioned."

"Fine. I don't know if I've got time for a quick snog round the back of the church with a fit-looking painter."

"So, you think he's fit then?"

Penny laughed. "Give over. Solve a murder first and then you can start interfering in my love life."

"It's a deal," said Izzy.

"What? No. Wait. I didn't mean it like that."

Izzy stood and tucked the sketch book under her arm.

41

On Wednesday morning, Izzy rode her colourful yarn-wrapped bicycle down the path alongside the old cemetery to Annalise's house on Fairfield Crescent. Annalise lived in a narrow, modern terraced house. Its white-painted walls were flaking and smudged with patches of mould. Lichen gathered around the low roof edge and gutters. The front garden was tiny and empty apart from a handful of anaemic potted plants, a pair of garden gnomes and a pottery hedgehog.

The doorbell didn't seem to be working so Izzy knocked. A shadow appeared at the frosted glass and the door opened. It was Pam, Annalise's mum, wearing a pair of yellow washing-up gloves and a rather terse expression.

"Oh," she said, in mild surprise. "Hello."

"Sorry." Izzy looked at the gloves. "Am I interrupting?"

"Laundry day. You after Annalise? Is this newspaper business?"

"No, I'm..." Izzy held up Merida's tote bag, and if the sun didn't quite rise over Pam's hard expression, it at least warmed a few degrees.

"She forgot it, didn't she? Even though she had a lovely time. And you knew it was hers?"

"The snowflakes. A bit of a Frozen fan."

"Who isn't?" said Pam. "What girl doesn't dream of heading off into the wilderness and making herself a magic ice castle without needing to worry about mortgages and rent, eh?" She made to take it from Izzy, realised her gloved hands were wet, and then gestured inside. "D'you fancy a cup of tea?"

"Don't mind if I do," said Izzy and stepped inside.

The house was filled with the smell of laundry and Izzy was at once reminded of the open-top twin-tub washing machine Nanna Lem used to have in her back scullery. The thick soapy smell wasn't something you encountered often these days.

"Washing machine broke down," said Pam, gesturing at the sink in the tub filled with wet laundry. "Repairing the old one will cost money we just don't have. And the laundrette's a rip-off. So we're having to make do until pay day comes around."

"You live here too?" asked Izzy. She hadn't known.

Pam pulled off a glove with an audible snap. "Just temporarily. Need to find another job." She clicked on the kettle and saw Izzy looking at her. "Oh, we'll cope just fine. Something always comes along in times of trouble. If life has taught me anything it's self-reliance."

With her gloves off, Pam was able to take the tote bag

from Izzy. She ran her fingers over the stitched-on snowflakes.

"I'm insanely proud of that little girl. I know grandmas should be."

"She's got a fine eye for design," Izzy agreed honestly.

"She's clever, too. And her mum is. Again, self-reliant." Pam picked up two cups from the draining board and rubbed them inside and out with a tea towel before taking them over to the kettle.

"Do you not have a high opinion of Annalise's husband?" said Izzy.

Pam laughed. "He's fine enough. He loves them both, which is apparently all you can expect of a bloke these days. Still don't see why she had to marry him. A mug's game."

"I like a nice wedding. It's traditional."

Pam scoffed as she poured teas. "White dresses as some stupid symbol of purity. Your old dad giving you away like you're his property. And that love, honour and obey rubbish. At least Annalise had the sense to go for a simple registry office wedding. She wore this wonderful emerald green dress. Stunning. Of course, you appreciate a nice dress."

"I do."

Pam opened a drawer to get a teaspoon. The drawer jammed and she had to fight viciously to get it to close again.

"I was hoping to see Annalise. I wanted to ask about the obituaries we were going to write for the paper," said Izzy.

"Obituaries? Oh. Them two. Annalise is snowed under at work without them. Ipswich head library have told her they're sending over some help but it doesn't seem to have materialised yet."

"Of course, you were both there on the night Roy died." Izzy felt very self-conscious dropping this into the conversation. It felt hugely clumsy, and she feared Pam would immediately call her out for her snooping.

"Where? Oh, the library. We were. They don't know how he died yet, do they? I mean, like where and when he poisoned himself."

"I heard someone say it was the champagne."

"What? Stuart Dinktrout trying to poison us all with cheap fizz? Can't be that. We all drank from the same bottle."

"Who poured it out?"

Pam's eyes narrowed in suspicion. "Annalise helped me with the drinks. I was with her the whole time. Roy was a horrid specimen of a man. All..." She made spidery creepy fingers in the air. "But my Annalise is a lovely person, nothing but genuine care for others in her heart. Too keen to help, sometimes. I know who I blame."

"You do?" said Izzy.

"Lorina Reid. If it wasn't for her, I reckon Roy Cotwin would still be alive."

"But Lorina's dead."

"Doesn't mean she isn't responsible," said Pam with considerable venom. "One of those two would have killed the other eventually."

42

Penny loved Framlingham. It was something she hadn't really considered in her time away. In her absence, she had forgotten the charm and the sense of community that could build up around a place, how special events and local achievements were more notably marked in a town like this, that it was a place with its own character, where life didn't pass you by, leaving you untouched and anonymous. That being said, spending an afternoon looking through page after page of local history books was more than a little tedious.

Here, the Boxing Day fox hunt coming cantering through the town. Here, a drayman's cart parked outside the Crown Inn. Here, the White Horse pub, long since closed. Here, a saddlemaker in his apron standing proudly outside his workshop. Here, the windmill out by Saxtead Green. Image after image, name after name.

Penny went up to the counter.

Annalise had a library book open in front of her and was scanning the barcode stuck into the title page. Her fingers rested lightly on the felt tip and biro marks left by readers in the corner of the page. She realised Penny was watching her.

"Going to be a long time before Lorina's ghost leaves this place," she said.

Penny nodded in understanding. "Izzy tells me that you keep back issues of the Frambeat Gazette."

"We do. Over this way."

She showed Penny the filing box containing the amateur local paper. "We've got the original desktop publishing files somewhere if you'd like it in electronic format. And we've got digitised copies of all the major Suffolk papers."

"No, that's great," said Penny. She looked at the most recent issue on the top. Below the World Book Day headline was a picture of Annalise's own daughter, dressed in cobwebs and a taken-up white wedding dress and clutching a copy of *Great Expectations*.

"A costume choice Lorina would have approved of," Annalise noted. "Is there anything in particular you were looking for?"

"Izzy said that there was an interview with Stuart Dinktrout or a profile or something."

"Ah, yes. Middle of last year, I think." Her dextrous fingers riffled through copies and came up with an edition from the previous summer. "Here."

There was a picture of Stuart, in a tweedy waistcoat, chest puffed out proudly.

"Rather, um, full of himself," Annalise suggested. "But a fixture in the town."

"Oh, I remember Dinktrout's from my own childhood," said Penny.

"My mum knew him of old. Lorina too. Think they were all at school together. She was quite sweet on him at one point."

Penny recalled the conversation she had overheard between Stuart and Lorina shortly before her death. It hadn't sounded like there was much sweetness left between them.

"Thanks for this," she said and went back to the non-fiction section to sit down and read it.

The article was little more than a puff piece, an interview in which Stuart Dinktrout got to share his thoughts on how important he and his business were to the local area. There was much to be learned from it, though. The Dinktrout Rose, white with the red-frilled edges, was a unique cultivar that was now exported across Europe and even to America. Stuart's grandfather had gained Plant Breeder's Rights, a sort of copyright for plants, back in the nineteen-thirties, and was recognised on the national list in the same decade. That meant that, for a long time, no one was allowed to sell or propagate that rose without his permission. Penny found it quite astonishing that one could own the rights to the genes of a living thing but there it was, in black and white.

Stuart's interview went on to expound on the other ventures at Dinktrout's Nursery. The petting zoo and the restaurant café got a mention. He managed to slip in a reference to their two-for-one Sunday lunch OAP special offer, a blatant piece of self-advertising that even mentioned how they were keeping their prices down while the local pubs were raising theirs.

It was at that moment that a flash of recollection struck her. It was an image of prices, a bill of sale. And it was in the book that Lorina had insisted Penny borrow.

"Oh, heck!" she said out loud.

"Is everything okay?" Annalise called from the front desk.

Hurriedly, with panicked hands, Penny shoved the books she'd been looking at back onto the shelves and dropped the copy of the Frambeat Gazette back at the counter.

"Is everything okay?" Annalise asked again.

"I know why Stuart did it!" said Penny, feeling her chest constricted with excitement and nerves.

"Did what?" said Annalise but Penny was already hurrying out, down the lane and back to the shop.

43

When Izzy got back to the shop, she saw Penny had the thin volume *Framlingham's History in Pictures* open on the counter and was holding her phone over it.

"Solved it!" Penny declared.

"Have you now?" said Izzy.

"Well, half of it."

"Which half?"

"The bit where Stuart Dinktrout killed Lorina Reid."

"Oh."

Penny fiddled with her phone, and gave a dry chuckle when it pinged. She turned the book round on the counter to show Izzy.

"I've sent Stuart the evidence and he's told me he's coming straight down here. You've got maybe ten minutes to see if you can spot it."

"Spot what?"

Penny tapped the history book. "It's the secret Lorina knew that was genuinely worth killing her for."

Izzy looked at the history book. On the two-page spread she could see photos of tradesmen in the marketplace, a picture of an old horse and cart, and a hand-written receipt for various items, the prices marked out in pounds, shillings and pence. Izzy's eyes flicked across it all, not sure what she was supposed to see. A weapon? A motive written in huge bold letters?

She paused.

"So you invited the murderer here?" she asked.

"I... did," said Penny. "Ooh, do you think that was a bad idea?"

"I'm not sure I want to be alone in a shop when an accused murderer turns up."

"You'll be with me."

"I still think that's a bit too alone, don't you?"

Izzy took her phone out. "I'm messaging Tariq. He wanted proof we didn't do it. Maybe I should tell Pam."

"Why Pam?"

"She was absolutely convinced that Lorina killed Roy. Maybe she was right, maybe Lorina really did kill Roy because he was forcing her out, and then Stuart killed Lorina for entirely unrelated reasons." Messages sent, Izzy returned her attention to the book. "Is it this list of things sold to Dinktrout's Nursery?"

"It is," said Penny.

"But it's stuff sold to Stuart's granddad, not Stuart."

"And what's in the list?"

The list was written in that weird sloping hand that oldytimey accountants seemed to favour and was full of abbreviations which made it even harder to read.

"*Smple Winter Pomery app. saplings x six*," she read. "*Two x gross pot. seedlings internat. kidney.* Lord knows what that is. *Four x rose bushes (whit & red petals).*"

"There you go," said Penny.

"Internat kidney?"

"No. The roses."

There was a real-life squeal of brakes, and a black prestige car rocked against the kerb outside.

"He did drive quickly," said Penny.

"He's here?" said Izzy.

"I might have made a mistake in taunting him."

"Did you taunt him?"

"I did sort of dangle the evidence in his face."

A flustered-looking Stuart Dinktrout almost fell out of his car, took a second to compose himself and hurried to the shop door.

He burst in, very much out of breath, and his eyes latched onto Penny.

"Who have you told?"

"Don't try anything funny. We've called the police," Izzy lied.

Stuart's brow creased deeply, as if she had said the most stupid thing. "The police?"

"We know everything," said Izzy airily.

He strode to the counter, grasped the book and stared at it. He flipped to the front cover, made a frustrated sound and then opened it again and put his hand on the picture of the sales receipt.

"I've been looking for this for months. Lorina was practically waving it in front of me."

"She'd been dropping heavy hints," said Penny. "Had you checking all the local history books."

"She thought it was a bloody game."

Izzy leaned over to Penny and whispered, "I still don't see what it is."

Penny tapped the book. "The key to the Dinktrout fortune. The Dinktrout Rose."

Izzy blinked. "The four times rose bushes with red and white petals?"

"Stuart's grandfather claimed to have cultivated it himself and registered plant breeder's rights."

"Whereas the originator was this chap?"

Stuart squinted at the name at the top of the document. "PW Rogerson."

"Who is that?" asked Izzy.

"No idea," Stuart admitted. "I've never heard of Rogerson. But it's not *Dinktrout*, is it?"

Izzy was frowning. She still didn't understand.

"Imagine if this got out," continued Stuart. "It wouldn't be the Dinktrout Rose any more. It would be something else. The *Rogerson* Rose, maybe." Izzy thought the words had a certain ring to them, but from the way Stuart sniffed contemptuously as he spoke them, she suspected he didn't agree. "Horrible," he said. "That rose is what the public associates with the Dinktrout name. And then there's all the people who paid for a licence to sell the rose decades ago. Who knows what they'd do? Or what the descendants of this Rogerson would do? It might be grounds for them to sue. It could ruin us. And after all the good we've done for the local area."

"Reason enough for you to have killed Lorina Reid," Penny nodded.

Stuart's gaze was both furious and uncomprehending. "What?"

"She threatened to expose you, didn't she? Was she actually blackmailing you or did she just do it out of some perverse sort of fun? I heard you arguing in the library."

"We were friends!"

"And," said Penny, in the manner of one who had just remembered something, "I heard her say she knew what you were up to with the rosé fizz. Did you agree to poison Roy for her in exchange for the incriminating book?"

"What madness is this?" he said, propelling himself away from the counter. "I thought..." His head twitched from Penny to Izzy and back again. "I thought you were just talking about the pictures. Did you actually think I killed someone?"

"Lorina died in your garden centre, after she had been heard saying she was going there specifically to see you," said Penny.

"And you didn't like the colour of Roy's house," added Izzy.

"Well, no. It was bloody ugly. I —"

He was interrupted by the sound of the door opening. Tariq entered first, followed by Pam Ockenden and Annalise.

"What's this about solving murders?" asked Annalise.

"Who told you?" said Izzy.

"I had a message from our over-excited student reporter and then a phone call from Mum."

"Oh, God, is everyone here?" cried Stuart.

"Got to say, the shop's never been busier," said Izzy.

"Whatever accusations are being flung around, neither Glenmore nor myself will allow them to be printed in the Frambeat Gazette," said Annalise. She spotted the latest copy on the counter and snatched it up. "World Book Day costumes and humorously shaped vegetables and an article on people's favourite scissors. That's what the Frambeat Gazette is about."

"People's favourite scissors?" asked Stuart.

"Fabric scissors," said Izzy. "People have been sharing them on social media." She flicked through her phone to find the images to show him.

"These fools," said Stuart, "think I murdered Roy Cotwin. Just because I brought the champagne that evening. Which is impossible because I didn't give him his glass and they were all the same."

Penny shook her head.

"No?" said Stuart.

"We were all there that night. I mean Izzy wasn't and Tariq wasn't." She closed her eyes and stretched out her hands.

"Ooh, she's picturing the scene," said Izzy.

"The cork was popped, fizz splashed about and I spoke to Roy and then the champagne appeared and..." She held out her hand. "The glasses had straws in them."

"Straws are fun," said Pam.

"I have a poisoned straw theory," said Izzy.

"No, it's simpler than that," said Penny.

"Are we actually going to find out who did it?" asked Tariq. "Because I really did call the police."

"Bloody waste of time, this," said Stuart.

"Izzy thought one of the straws itself might be poisoned," said Penny. "She did a little demonstration here with three glasses and put sugar as the poison in one of the glasses."

"It wasn't real poison," Izzy clarified. "The sugar was pretending to be poison."

"And then Lorina came into the shop. At that moment. It was the day she died. She came in and she saw the glasses and took one and she drank the one with sugar in, remember?"

"I do."

"And why did she drink the one with sugar in?"

"Random chance," said Annalise.

"No. She picked the one with blue straw."

"Blue was her favourite colour," said Pam.

"And on the night of Roy's death, there was a glass with a blue straw in it."

"No, they all had straws in," said Stuart. "Some others were blue, weren't they?"

"Yes, because..." Penny gave a sudden and inappropriate burst of laughter. "It's like the codes in the books. Annalise, at the library."

"Codes?"

"Yes. The people who read lots of books leave their own secret marks in books and Lorina's method of combating that was to make identical marks in all the books. If every book has a special mark in it, then effectively none of them do. The murderer had time to put the rat poison from under the sink in one glass, and mark it with a straw, but then another person, possibly being helpful, decided to put straws in all the drinks. The marked drink was no longer marked."

"So it was random?" said Tariq.

"Yes — Oh." Penny looked momentarily queasy. "Roy took two glasses and passed one to me. It was pure chance he didn't give me the poisoned glass."

"Hang on," said Tariq, "if one glass was initially marked with a blue straw then that would mean Lorina was the intended victim all along."

"It would," Penny conceded.

"Lorina's actual murder was just a second attempt. And no one actually wanted to kill Roy."

"I think there were some people who were glad he was dead," said Penny, and there were suddenly a couple of ashamed-looking faces in the room.

"But I still don't see how anyone could have planned that murder," said Stuart. "I know I didn't poison anyone, and no one knew I was bringing champagne."

"So, it was a spur of the moment decision," said Izzy.

"Who decides to try to murder someone in the middle of a retirement do?"

"Because they heard something said that night."

"Lorina said something worth killing her over?" said Stuart, scoffing.

"She gave that speech," said Annalise. "A nice little speech about all the kindnesses she'd done over the years. Helping customers, returning lost cheques, posting letters left in books. Something about bacon used as bookmarks, I can't recall."

Izzy's eyes fell onto the copy of the Frambeat Gazette in Annalise's hand and the photograph on the front page of a little girl in her World Book Day costume.

"It's Miss Havisham!" she said, in a voice far louder than she intended.

Annalise frowned and looked at the newspaper. "Yes, it is. Her teachers thought it was a very imaginative costume."

"No, no, it's..." Izzy gripped her hair in both hands. Thoughts and questions and, most importantly, answers were suddenly coursing through her noggin. She stabbed a finger at Stuart.

"You love that pig, don't you?"

"Er. If you mean I'm fond of dear Arabella, then..."

Izzy pointed at Annalise. "You got married in a green dress!"

"Yes. Is that relevant?"

Izzy's finger turned to Pam. "You said Roy's death was Lorina's fault!"

"Did I?" said Pam.

"Many many years ago, you were engaged, weren't you, Stuart?"

"I was," he said.

"To Pam. Pam, that's your white wedding dress in the picture. The one you never got to wear."

"You say it like it's a surprise," said Stuart.

"I think we all knew that," said Annalise. "I knew that."

"It was a long time ago," added Pam. "All in the past."

"You bought a wedding dress but never got to wear it. You

never married Stuart. You never married into the Dinktrout fortune."

"Pam broke it off," said Stuart. "As she said, it's all in the past. It's no use going back to yesterday, because I was a different person then."

"All in the past, but Pam held onto the dress."

"Please, don't," said Pam. "This is very upsetting."

But Izzy wasn't ready to stop. "When I was doing Arabella's waistcoat fitting, Stuart, you said your bride-to-be had broken off the engagement by letter. So impersonal. A letter."

Penny's eyes widened. Yes, Izzy could see that she now understood, too.

"I wonder when you wrote that letter, Pam," said Penny. "How early in the engagement that was. I bet it was a long time before the wedding. Maybe some early nerves."

"No, I only received it a few days before the wedding," said Stuart.

"Shortly after Lorina posted it. Yes."

Annalise's face fell. "Her speech. She found a forgotten letter in a book and popped it in the post box. You mean, Mum didn't mean to...?"

"Things said in a letter written ages previously," explained Penny. "You wrote the words and tucked them away in a book. And maybe your nerves eased or you became reconciled to the wedding and one way or another, you were all set to go ahead with it, but then the letter was found and sent by helpful Lorina and read only a scant few days before the wedding," said Penny. "The unexpected hurt caused. The confusion. Maybe you tried to explain to Stuart but it was a surprise and an upset. Best postpone the whole thing."

"You never married the richest man in town," said Izzy.

"And he never found anyone to replace you," said Penny.

"That sadness. The bitterness."

"Lorina revealed all this in one line of her speech. Then the champagne was opened. Pam, you took it into the kitchen. You must have been very angry. And there was the rat poison. And a blue straw to mark the glass you were putting it in."

"You must have had very little time. A minute or two at most."

"But then Annalise came along and started sticking straws in all the others," said Penny. "The identified glass of fizz became one among many. Not just one blue straw."

"You're saying this is my fault?" said Annalise.

"No," said Izzy, firmly. "As Pam herself said, Lorina was responsible. With one single act of helpfulness all those years ago, she set events in motion."

"No wonder you were so upset when you heard Roy was dead," Penny said to Pam. "You had no idea who you had poisoned or if you had even successfully poisoned anyone."

"No, it's not like that," said Pam and there were tears in her eyes.

"You can't prove my mum did any of this," said Annalise, putting an arm around the sagging woman's shoulder.

"I can prove one thing," said Izzy, holding out her phone. "Pam posted a picture of pink shears on social media. Still in the packet, you'll notice. And I saw those shears at Dinktrout's."

"We could check the timestamp of the photo," said Tariq.

"And probably place you at the garden centre at the time of Lorina's murder."

Pam shook her head. "I saw her there by accident. I didn't follow her."

"Mum, shush now," said Annalise.

"And Lorina was so full of herself. Off to see Stuart with an armful of bloody history books. Going to *help him out*, she said."

There was a flash of light and Izzy looked round to see a police car drawing up at the roadside behind Stuart's car. Tariq really had called the police.

Pam sniffed back tears. "Lorina Reid. Bloody helping people. Ruining lives."

The shop door opened. There were bootsteps on the dark wood floor.

"Just think how things could have been," Pam said. "If everybody minded their own business, the world would go around a great deal better than it does."

44

A trip from Framlingham to St Agnes' hospital in Ipswich was only twenty miles but it was an hour's journey on the bus. It wended through Earl Soham, Helmingham, Ashbocking, and Witnesham, between fields just beginning to show off the new spring's growth.

"I suppose," said Izzy thoughtfully, "that it must have been Pam herself who was out and about in town and heard you making the call to the police tip line."

"I guess," said Penny.

"She knew the library. Nipped upstairs, took the rat poison and binned it somewhere."

"Hard to believe she did it, really."

"Spur of the moment," said Izzy. "We sometimes make rash decisions."

Penny hummed in thought. "Like agreeing to give up a perfectly good job in London hotel in order to help run a down-at-heel sewing shop."

"I thought you were fired or something."

"Shush you," Penny smiled.

"You going to tell me what happened with your la-di-da London job?"

"Maybe one day."

At St Agnes', they found Nanna Lem in the lounge with the spectacular view over the wide River Orwell.

She saw them and waved a piece of toast at them.

"Look at that," she said.

"It's toast," Penny replied, not sure there was anything else to be said on the matter.

"How hard can it be to make sure the butter is evenly spread across the toast?"

"Says a woman who has people bringing plates of toast to her."

Nanna Lem gave her a critical look. "You saying beggars can't be choosers?"

Penny said nothing. Izzy bent over the side of the chair and planted a big kiss on the old woman's cheek.

"How's the leg?" said Izzy.

"Feels fine. These pink pills the doctors have got me on are doing wonders."

"I thought you were on orange pills," said Penny.

"Seems I was enjoying the orange pills too much as well. How's my two favourite grandchildren?"

"Favourites?" said Izzy.

Nanna Lem coughed. "— grandchildren who are currently present and in earshot."

Izzy grinned.

"More importantly," said Nanna Lem. "How's my shop?"

"Still upright," Penny told her.

"Penny's made some alterations," said Izzy.

"Exterior repainted. At no cost to you," Penny added.

"And she took down your reasons to murder customers sign," said Izzy.

"What she do that for?" asked Nanna Lem.

"Thought it set the wrong tone," said Izzy.

"Did she now?"

"And she's right," said Izzy firmly. "Penny has some good ideas about how the place should be run. We've tidied up the workshop and put on a kid's sewing workshop."

"Oh?" said Nanna Lem, surprised. "So you've enjoyed a spot of sewing then, Penny?"

Penny tilted her head. "The shop and the town have certain charms." She felt certain that Izzy was about to say something crass and unnecessary about a local painter and decorator so quickly added, "You on the mend then, Nanna?"

Nanna Lem waggled her toes in her support boot. "Doctors aren't one hundred percent sure that I'm right as rain yet. And they need to do one of them assessments to see if I can look after myself."

"Oh," said Izzy, in a sad tone that was not at all convincing. "Are you telling us that Penny will have to stay in Fram and keep helping me run the shop?"

Nanna Lem gave Izzy a shrewd look and then looked at Penny. "I mean, if she's willing..."

"I mean, I might need to start drawing a salary out of the shop's profits, if there are any," said Penny.

Nanna Lem shrugged. "It makes no odds to me. You think

I'm interested in the money? If I'd wanted a life of luxury, I'd have married a rich farmer." She blew out her lips. "More to life than that, eh?"

"I reckon so," said Penny.

Nanna Lem bit deeply into her toast and chewed. "In that case, I'd be delighted if you stayed on for a bit."

Penny nodded and could see out of the corner of her eye that Izzy was grinning like a fool.

"As long as you two don't get into no trouble," said the old woman.

Penny and Izzy exchanged glances. "Trouble? Us?"

ABOUT THE AUTHOR

Millie Ravensworth writes the Cozy Craft Mystery series of books. Her love of murder mysteries and passion for dressmaking made her want to write books full of quirky characters and unbelievable murders.

Millie lives in central England where children and pets are something of a distraction from the serious business of writing, although dog walking is always a good time to plot the next book.

If you visit www.pigeonparkpress.com/montys-party you can find a bonus story about when Penny and Izzy organise a sewing party for a group of boys and a very naughty dog.

ALSO BY MILLIE RAVENSWORTH

The Painted Lobster Murders

A quirky and funny series for fans of a good mystery and compelling characters. Can you solve the crime before our dressmaking duo?

Penny Slipper runs a sewing shop in the beautiful market town of Framlingham and she's got her wild and creative cousin, Izzy, to help with the latest dressmaking project.

A classic car weekend is coming to town and stylish Fliss Starling wants an outfit that will match her husband's elegant vintage car.

When one of Fliss's house guests is murdered by a masked intruder, Penny and Izzy have a deadly mystery to solve (as well as a dress to make!). With the aid of a cheeky little corgi dog and handyman Aubrey, they begin to search out the clues to this motor-related murder.

But fingers are soon pointing at Penny and Izzy when the intruder's mask appears to have come from their own shop! And rival shop owner, Carmella, would be delighted to see them take the blame.

Can Penny and Izzy stitch the pieces of this puzzle together and find the guilty culprit?

If you enjoy fast-paced mysteries, charming country towns and characters who you want to spend hours with then you're going to love the Cozy Craft Mystery series.

Start your next murder mystery adventure today!

The Painted Lobster Murders

The Sequined Cape Murders

Cozy Craft Mysteries can be read in any order. A funny whodunnit series, full of charming characters and mysteries that will keep you guessing to the very end.

Things are going great for Penny Slipper. Running a sewing shop in the middle of the English countryside is like a dream come true and she's got her colourful cousin Izzy and her corgi, Monty, to keep her entertained.

Her grandma's eightieth birthday is coming up soon and Penny and Izzy are busier than ever, making fancy dress costumes for the party guests.

However, Penny's dream life is thrown into chaos when a murdered woman is found in the bathroom of her cosy flat above the shop. With the doors and the windows all locked, no one can understand how this mystery corpse got there.

But things take a further sinister turn when a local shopkeeper is also killed. There's a murderer on the loose and no one is safe!

Can Penny and Izzy uncover the answers and unmask the criminal in their midst?

If your ideal book features mystery, friendship, cute romance, even cuter animals, crafting and a big slice of birthday cake then this is the book for you.

The Sequined Cape Murders

The Swan Dress Murders

Cozy Craft Mysteries can be read in any order. A funny whodunnit series, full of charming characters and mysteries that will keep you guessing to the very end.

A wedding is a cause for celebration. Not only do dressmakers Penny and Izzy get an invite to the big day but they have an unusual dress commission to complete for one of the guests.

It seems Penny's only problem is deciding which potential boyfriend to take as her plus-one guest — practical handyman Aubrey or cultured fabric expert Oscar.

But bigger problems arise when the maker of the wedding cake is found dead in the grounds of the stately home where the wedding is to take place.

And when another key individual in the wedding plans is also murdered, it seems like someone has deadly plans to prevent this marriage.

Can Penny and Izzy unravel the mystery and solve this crime before the big day is fatally ruined?

If your ideal book features mystery, friendship, cute romance, crafting and a charming rural setting then this is the book for you.

The Swan Dress Murders

Printed in Great Britain
by Amazon